EMMA'S FORLORN HOPE

ELLA CORNISH

This is a work of fiction. Any names or characters, businesses or places, events or incidents, are fictitious. Any resemblance to actual persons, living or dead, or actual events is purely coincidental.

Copyright © 2020 by Ella Cornish

All rights reserved.

No part of this book may be reproduced in any form or by any electronic or mechanical means, including information storage and retrieval systems, without written permission from the author, except for the use of brief quotations in a book review.

Email: ellacornishauthor@gmail.com

CHAPTER 1

*R*ain fell hard against the windowpanes, the thick splatters sounding like gunshots in the quiet and dark of the house. Though it was day, the ashen grey clouds blanketed the world like a death shroud. There was a chill in the air, a driving wind clawing its way through the cracks in the stonework and whistling like angered banshees through the house. The raging elements made it hard to think and Emma Moss could not have been more thankful for it. Thinking was the last thing she wanted, as was silence. For the last two days, the house had been quiet as the grave and she could hardly stand it. Angry though the elements were, their raging cacophony was welcome to the nothingness that had taken over her home.

Sat in the rocking chair at her mother's bedside, Emma stared blankly at the windows, watching them rattle whilst trying to count each raindrop. Dark rings circled her eyes and her cheeks were stained with the dried-up channels of tears that no longer flowed. Wrapped in an old, frayed shawl, Emma barely noticed the cold. She was far too numb.

By her side, Emma's mother lay silent and quiet in the bed, covered in as many layers of blankets as Emma could find about the house. She would have had a fire going, except water had gotten to the logs. She hadn't bothered to complain to Father. Since Mother had fallen ill, the man had come undone. Though never very reliable to begin with, Thomas Moss was nothing without his wife. He was a boat and she the rudder. Emma was told it had always been so, and that her father would never have amounted to anything in life without her mother's influence. Now, as the woman they both loved lay silent and dying in her bed, Emma felt she truly understood the kind of man her father was. Content to wallow in ennui and self-pity, he had holed himself away in the quiet corners of the house for the past days, never once looking to cook for or check after his children. Emma had to ride out to the wet nurse in the nearby village to beg her care for her young sister for a few days, and she was glad she had done so. If left under her father's watch, Emma was certain baby Mary would have been left to starve.

As dissatisfied thoughts of her father swirled through her head, Emma let out a sigh. She tried to ignore the dark and empty fireplace and instead thought about slipping beneath the covers of her mother's bed. Their combined warmth would do them both good, she thought.

With nothing to be done until dinner and the doctor's next visit, Emma made up her mind. Rising up from the chair, the floor creaked loudly underfoot as she moved around the bed and slipped beneath the patchwork covers. She had hoped she was quiet enough not to disturb her mother's rest, but she felt a stirring beneath the sheets as she lay down next to the woman who had raised and nurtured her.

"Thomas… Is that you? Finally risked coming back to your own bed?"

"No, Mama, it's me," Emma spoke softly. She heaved a sigh as she turned her head into the pillows. She wanted to apologise for her father never being there, but it was not her crime to apologise for.

"Your father still sitting in the living room? If he's not careful he'll run out of chances to see me," Mrs Moss said, her voice a pitiful whisper.

"Don't speak like that Mother," Emma said, pushing in a little closer and wrapping her arms around the woman who had raised her.

"Where's Mary?" Mrs Moss asked, before descending into a fit of coughing. Emma sat up and passed over a pewter cup of water. Her mother swallowed a few grateful sips then coughed again.

As Emma took back the glass, she could not help but notice the flecks of blood on the rim of the cup. "Where's Mary?" the woman asked again.

"I told you last time you woke, I sent her to Elsie Brown, the wet nurse. She's promised to look after Mary at no charge until you get better."

"Does she know that'll mean adopting her?" Mrs Moss asked, her gallows humour earning no laugh from her daughter.

The room fell to silence once more, mother and daughter both lying wrapped up together and listening to the sound of the driving rain. Emma held her mother tight in her arms, possessively.

"You know you can't afford to be like your

father," Emma heard her mother say, her voice softer.

"Mother?"

"You can't keep going through life finding ways to pretend everything is fine when the house is burning down around you."

"I don't think there is any chance of that with all this rain," Emma joked, trying desperately to deflect her mother's message.

"You know what I mean, Emma," her mother said. She turned now, staring into her eldest daughter's eyes. It was the most alert and together she had seemed in days and yet Emma felt a shudder pass through her as she studied her mother's face. It was so sallow, her skin like paper hanging off her bones. Her hair was limp and lifeless, and she just seemed exhausted—thoroughly and completely. "I want to know that you will look after Mary," the woman continued. There was an edge to her voice, her request one that Emma could not dismiss or bat aside with empty assurances.

"Will you look after Mary when I am gone, Emma?" her mother asked again. Beneath the sheets, her hands moved to find her daughter's, winding their fingers together and grasping tight. "I need to know that you won't abandon her or let anything bad happen to her. I... I love your father, but I know what he is like, too. He won't be any good at all when I'm gone. I need to know I can rely on you to look after yourself and your sister."

Emma bit her bottom lip. She thought she was done with crying. In the last days she had shed so many tears she felt certain she had nothing left to give. Still, as she tried to summon up the words to answer her mother, she felt the familiar dampness on her cheeks, the hateful blurring at the edges of her vision. She couldn't refuse to answer her mother, at the same time she wanted so desperately to ignore the question. Emma couldn't explain it, but she felt at that moment as if she had the power over life and death with her answer. It felt like her mother was asking for her permission to die, ready to slip away once Emma gave her the assurance that she needed to enter that last and deepest of rests.

"Mother, I..."

"Please, Emma," the woman begged again, her dull eyes staring intently at her.

"You know I won't let anything happen to Mary," Emma said at last. The words were halting, broken between half sobs as she nestled into her mother and rested her head in the crook of her neck.

"That's my good girl," came a voice that seemed

eerily peaceful and distant. Emma took deep lungfuls of air as she tried to calm herself. No further words passed between them. Emma did not know what else to say, only able to communicate her feelings by the way she held fast to her mother in the dark.

~

Her eyes flickered open. Outside, the rain had eased to a dull drizzle and the wind calmed to a respectful whisper. It was later than Emma had expected it to be. The bedroom was swathed in darkness and there was no light from under the door frame. The dark clouds of day had drawn into a night, black as pitch, and Emma could hardly even make out her mother's form in the bed. Even without sight, Emma felt something was wrong.

Her mother was still, her body limp in a way that didn't feel like sleep. Emma's hand ran down her mother's arm, moving to her wrist to check for a pulse. For a moment, Emma's whole body tensed, and her lips pursed with worry. Her eyes stared into the dark ahead of her, unfocused and empty as she confirmed her suspicions.

Although there had been weeks to prepare and days to contemplate the possibility of her mother's death, Emma had put it off. Lying next to the unmoving and silent body, she felt as if she should feel something. She should start to cry again, wrap her arms about her mother and hold her as grief took over. Those felt like the right and natural things to do, but Emma found no compulsion or desire to do either.

Instead, she sat up. Sat up and pulled herself out of bed, taking a moment to light the nearby candle on the bedside table. In the faint illumination, she busied herself. She straightened the bed sheets and turned her mother so that she lay flat on her back with hands clasped together over her chest. This done, Emma found her shoes and slipped them on.

Stepping out into the hall, the girl found no light shining anywhere in the house. She held the candle in her hand firmly as she walked through to the living area and kitchen. There was a weak two-day-old broth in one of the pans left for them to eat. It was not much, but it would do until she could go out to the town in the morning. Finding the last of the coal in the kitchen, Emma set about lighting the stove, making a mental note of all that would need doing the next day.

There was the undertaker to inform and the parish priest. Doctor Philips would also need to know, and as Emma thought of the man, she wondered why he had not called as agreed. It did not matter much she told herself, focussing on what food she would need to purchase. How long could she leave Mary in the care of Mrs Brown? She had no doubt the kindly wet nurse would agree to look after her baby sister as long as was needed, but Emma couldn't take advantage of that generosity. Besides, she had promised mother that she would see to Mary.

The ongoing list of duties, responsibilities and plans marched on through Emma's mind as she stirred up the old broth in the pan. She stared into the liquid, hardly noticing as a shadow moved behind her. Only when the corner chair creaked did she realise her father had walked in. No doubt he could smell the food.

"How is she?" came the tentative question.

Emma almost didn't want to answer. She wasn't looking to spare her father's feelings or avoid the topic. Instead, she felt as though he had no right to know what had happened. He had chosen to lock himself away the last days and nights, resolutely shuttering the world out to wallow in self-pity. He didn't deserve to know anything. If he wanted to know he should march into his bedroom and see for himself.

"She's dead," Emma answered simply, knowing it would do no good to indulge in petty revenge. She stopped stirring the broth in the pan for a moment, listening for any sign of life or emotion behind her. She did not turn around though, not wishing to look her father in the eyes.

"Was it quick?" The man's voice was weak when he spoke, but Emma heard it.

"I don't know. I know she had fallen asleep. I closed my eyes to rest and when I woke again, she was gone." There was no emotion in her voice, just facts; as if she was telling the news of someone wholly unrelated to her.

For a few minutes, all was silent. Father said nothing, and Emma could not hear him stirring from his chair behind her. She continued with the cooking, stirring the remaining soup until it was bubbling hot. She then dished the meagre meal into two bowls and carried them over to the table. One she lay down before her father, not even looking him in the eyes as she did so. The other, she took to her own place.

"I'll need to see several people in town tomorrow," Emma said, her voice wooden and mechanical. "You'll need to see about going back to work soon. I can't look after Mary and go out to wash and clean for the Parr family."

"We'll move to the city," Thomas said, his voice matter of fact and strangely resolute. He too seemed numbed by everything, left empty and emotionless.

"The city?" Emma sucked in a breath, feeling a twinge of uncertainty. "Why would you say that?"

"It's where the work is," Thomas replied. "I can't expect to get anything here, not after what happened around the time your mother fell ill. Besides, I don't much feel like staying on in this place."

Emma took a sip of soup between pursed lips. "Do you know what you'd do in London?" she asked, trying to put on that voice her mother used to keep a check on him.

"I'll find something," he said, following the words up with a too-casual shrug.

And that was the end of it. Both numb, both unwilling or unable to grieve as they should, father and daughter ate their meal in silence, with the prospect of a new start in the city added to Emma's fears and uncertainties for the future.

CHAPTER 2

*L*ingering by the window, Emma wondered what use it even served. It afforded no view.

When they had first arrived in London, she had tried to keep a positive view on the move. She had accepted moving away from the family home and the country by reminding herself of all the amazing sights London had to offer. Of course, many of the sights Emma would have enjoyed were in the process of being rebuilt. Fires in the Palace of Westminster had destroyed much of parliament and were still being rebuilt, even a decade after. Trafalgar Square offered pleasing allure, as did the much-touted Great Exhibition in the Crystal Palace of Hyde Park. As Emma understood it, there was much to see, enjoy and experience in the capital, and her friends back home had expressed envy at her luck in travelling to the seat of power and culture in England.

However, the joys and delights of London were little more than candle beacons shining out amidst a labyrinth of tall, grey, smog blackened buildings and narrow choked alleyways. Their new home was tucked away in a gap between streets, its own little, squalid microcosm of poverty and wretchedness. Much of London was like this, Emma had learned. Those on the bottom rung were shepherded away to live in the crevices between streets. Whether long and narrow corridors or larger squares, these boltholes of the destitute were always hidden away behind the facades of better houses. It allowed the lords, ladies and affluent to wander the streets without having to face the ugly side of London life.

The window Emma sat by—the only window in the home—stared out at a section of grey, stone wall. If she moved down onto her knees and crooked her neck at an angle to look up, she could just about make out the skyline and the occasional shadows of sparrows and pigeons flying overhead. It depressed her to go to such lengths just to see the sun, but she sat by the window anyway. More often than not, her mind would conjure happier memories of the view from their old stone cottage out in the country. She remembered the light rolling hills that sloped gently down to the nearby town of Morton, the way the sky seemed to stretch on into infinity on cloudless summer days.

A sound brought her out of melancholy remembrance. The wistful look on Emma's face disappeared as her lips set into a hard line. She sucked in a deep breath as a cry from the crib behind her let her know that Mary was awake. Though it pained her not to run straight to her baby sister, Emma took a moment to compose herself. She had told herself that one of the things Mary needed most was to see her smiling. There had been few smiles since even before Mother had died, and Emma was determined to ensure that Mary was not brought up living in a world without joy. Even if she had to parrot the emotion, pretending that all was well, she would do it just to give the baby an extra sense of security and safety.

As she approached the cot, Emma leaned over with a slight rictus smile on her face.

"Hey, look who's awake," she said, reaching into the old drawer Emma had salvaged to use as a crib. She moved slowly, delicately lifting her baby sister from the bundle of rough woven sheets. Mary wailed loudly in her sister's ear, causing Emma to flinch at the sound. She tried to reason out in her head what the infant wanted, but her mind drew a blank. She was no mother and, more than this, she was tired. Since arriving in London, she was mother, housekeeper, cook and worker. They had only been in their home a few scant months and already the city had ground her under its merciless, industrial boot. Emma's eyes were ringed grey from a lack of sleep, and she yawned even as she tried to decide just what her demanding baby sister wanted now.

"Come on Mary," Emma cooed, her pleas close to whining. "I know you're hungry, but I can't give you anything till Father comes back."

Rocking Mary in her arms as she moved over to her own bed, Emma considered the advice Catherine, the mother next door, had offered her. Catherine was similarly overworked, frayed to her last nerve by demanding children and a husband who worked long hours in the factories. Her trick to getting her babies to behave themselves in the day was simply to let them cry until they lost their energy and found sleep. She had assured Emma that in a few short days Mary would learn never to bother crying for anything. It was a trick Emma found herself wanting to employ more and more as her spirit was broken down by work and tiredness, but always she resisted the urge.

Sitting back in the bed, resting Mary to her chest, Emma sung odd lullabies, her voice drowned out by the screaming of the child in her arms.

"Where is Father?" Emma asked herself aloud, no longer able to hide the agitation in her voice. Mary needed feeding and the shops would be closing soon. She had hoped to go out while her father watched Mary, but now she wondered if she would have to go out with Mary in tow.

Hunger and desperation won out. With the babe in her arms unwilling to wait for their absent father to return, it was on her to find them some food. Setting Mary down on the bed for a moment, Emma gathered her shoes and coat. She had kept a little of the money she had earned hawking for local traders hidden from her father, tucked away under a loose floorboard near the second-hand dresser. She bent down on hands and knees, flinching as she caught a splinter in her palm while lifting the loose beam of wood. She grabbed what was there, not bothering to count it, and tucked it into her pockets.

"We're almost ready, Mary, try and have a little more patience," Emma begged as she returned the board to its place and sucked her palm where the splinter stuck from her skin. Her little sister did not care for Emma's injury though, wailing louder and writhing on her back on the sheets. Emma put aside her efforts to suck out the slither of wood and moved over to the bed, picking up Mary and wrapping her a little tighter in the blankets. Emma had quickly become adept at tying Mary's bedclothes about her into a makeshift carrier. She felt bad binding the babe so tight to her chest, but she feared to wrap her up loosely in case she was to drop the child.

Stepping out from her home, Emma locked the door, not that there was anything left of value to steal in the upper floor room she called home. Their home was nothing more than a wooden extension hung from precarious scaffolding above one of the older stone buildings. Many homes in the Rookery were like this, limpets clinging to the backs of buildings, joined by wooden bridges, stairwells and a few by rope ladders.

Moving over the outer bridge, Emma took a care not to linger too near the railings. The wooden beam was rotted in a few places and she always feared her foot would smash through a worm-eaten board and falling to the hard-stone cobbles beneath. Once she made the stairs, Emma skittered down them quickly, feeling some relief as her feet touched the solid ground beneath her. In her arms, Mary was at last quieting. The baby nuzzled deep into Emma's chest, perhaps trying to seek out greater warmth from the autumn chill. She found little comfort in Mary's muffled whimpers and hurried out of the narrow Rookery she called home, striking out for the shops.

No sooner had Emma struck down the narrow alley toward the main streets than a figure blocked her path. The ways into the Rookery were narrow enough that residents typically had to walk in single file and, when undesirables wished to, it was easy to trap someone in the narrow, choked alleyway.

Emma sucked in a breath at the sight of the rather rotund figure who placed himself in her way. With his black coat, fine hat and pocket watch cord swaying proudly from his waistcoat pocket as he walked with purpose into the alley, it was obvious he was not the sort one could expect to find in the Rookeries. He was much too fine and affluent a man to have a residence in the cramped rooms tacked on to the backs of better buildings. He was more likely to be the owner and proprietor of those crumbling residences; a man whose comfort was supported by the misery he had others pay to endure.

"Mr Gulliver, my apologies," Emma said,

quickly backing up down the alley to let the man pass. Once out of the way, she kept her head bowed and held Mary closer to her upper body. She tried to make herself invisible as she waited for the man to pass. However, rather than moving past her to one of the houses, Gulliver stopped in place and turned smartly on his heels to look over her.

"You're Thomas Moss' girl, aren't you?" the man asked, voice low and eyes narrowing. Emma felt a sense of threat in the question and her eyes moved to the slender, black lacquered cane he held in his right hand. He did not need the thing for walking, and he gripped it in his hand the way one might wield a club or sword.

"I am Emma Moss, yes. I was just heading to the shops, I'm afraid my father is not at home." Emma spoke in a polite whisper, trying to decide if it showed better manners to look the man in the eye or avert her gaze as she spoke.

"Well, you can turn right back around and take me up to your house," Gulliver said, his voice authoritative and rough. With his stout, brick-like frame and monkey-like paws with thick knuckles, he had the look of a man you did not wish to cross. Despite Mary's muffled cries within her wrap,

Emma turned on her heel and moved toward the stairs.

"I will let you in, but then may I be excused; I really need—"

"—You'll stay girl," Gulliver said without a hint of apology or concern in his voice for the trouble he was causing her. "It is you I am here to see, anyway."

Gulliver's frank, almost dismissive words stopped Emma dead in her tracks, and she wheeled about on the stairs to look at him, brows knotted in confusion. "Me? Whatever could you want with me... sir?" She only barely remembered her politeness at the shock.

"Well, I was going to do this in the privacy of your home, but if you want all the neighbours to hear then that suits me just as well." Gulliver shrugged. "Your father took out a considerable loan with me when he came to the city and took on your home." Gulliver nodded to the wooden window box of a house. "It was agreed your father would pay this back within three months of settling in the city, with interest, of course."

"I know nothing of any of this," Emma replied, her voice defensive. Her lips pursed thin as she sucked in a breath. As Gulliver's words settled in her mind, she found it hard to deny them. She knew her father was bringing in money from somewhere on their arrival, but he had always been quite cagey on exactly what he was doing for work. Though she did not wish to, she could easily believe him of taking out a loan and sitting idly by on the cushion it provided until the hour of payment came."

"You do not seem too surprised by this news?" Gulliver probed. His head moved as he tried to catch Emma's eyes. She felt like he was a predator studying her for weakness, trying to find just the right angle from which to attack.

"I... I did not know anything about any loan, but I do know my father, sir. As much as I am loath to admit to it, I can well imagine his doing something like this." Emma sighed, her shoulders slumping. In her arms, Mary began to cry a little louder, tiny hands clutching at Emma's dress as though trying to console her in a hug. It took all of Emma's will power to keep tears of frustration from falling. "Regardless, everything I said before is true. My father is not home, and I do not know what time he will return. I am more than happy to let you inside to wait for him."

"Well, that's just the thing, my girl," Gulliver said, moving in close and putting one giant, bear-paw hand on her shoulder. "I have it on good authority from my associates that your father will not be coming home."

"Not coming... No... No, that I do not believe!" Emma tried to duck out of Gulliver's grasp, but the hand on her shoulder tightened its grip.

"My associates tried to have a gentle word with your father in one of the public houses quite a way out from here. It was strange to find Thomas there... almost like he was purposefully avoiding his home."

Emma kept her silence, pursing her lips and trying to resist showing any sign of pain as she struggled against the intensifying grip on her shoulder. Gulliver's look was getting more and more dangerous by the second, and his voice was turning to a bestial growl the longer he spoke.

"When my boys tried to talk with Thomas at the inn, do you know what he did? He ran, my girl. Your father ran like a rabbit spooked by the foxes. I'll give this much credit to your father, he's a slippery one. My boys never did quite work out where he went after that, but I think we can agree on one thing."

"What's that?" Emma asked, her teeth grinding together as she fought against the pain now shooting through her shoulder.

"You are in need of some assistance if you are to get by in this city."

Emma could have blinked, and she would have missed the change that suddenly came over Gulliver. All of a sudden, she was loosened from his vice-like grip. She was so unprepared that she staggered backwards, almost hitting the rotten railings on the stairs. It was Gulliver himself who saved her from going over, grabbing her by the waist and steadying her.

"My, don't you spook easily! Did you think you were in some kind of trouble for your father skipping out on his debt to us?" Gulliver's voice was now hearty, almost jolly, with a note of humour in his voice as he spoke.

"I am sorry if I offended," Emma said, feeling it would be unwise to try and answer the man's question in any way. Steady on her feet again, she rolled her hurting shoulder, the arm itself numb. With her right arm, she clutched Mary defensively, keeping her body slightly turned to Gulliver so her sister was shielded from him.

"I suppose I can't take offence when you have just been forced to hear such tragic news—learning your father has sold you out and run off to leave you alone to face his creditors. Of course, you would be nervous." Gulliver's act of caring and understanding was more unsettling than his angry side. There was something far more insidious, far more deceptive and concerning, about his sudden charitable understanding.

"I... I have a little money from my work I can use to go towards my father's debt," Emma said, trying to get to the heart of the matter.

"With the interest your father owes, together with the loan and rent on your home, I doubt very much that you stashed enough coins away to cover even a single measly percent of his debt." Gulliver still seemed oddly calm despite his grim assessment. "Besides, can you really afford to pay anything towards your father's debt when you have a little one to feed? This is your sister, right? You didn't... you didn't have a boy sweet on you out in the country leave you with this?"

"No! Certainly not!" Emma declared, disgusted that Gulliver would even consider such a thing.

"But I am right about the rest though, aren't I? You won't be able to keep your sister if I take your money and kick you both out on the streets. Your only hope would be to surrender her to the parish and hope they will take mercy on her. Very potluck —but when you have no other options before you, well..."

Emma knew she was being lured into a trap.

Gulliver was hardly being subtle in his routine. It was even possible he knew the strength of his position compared to Emma's—knew she would have little choice but to listen to any kind of a deal he might offer her.

"You seem to know better than I what might become of me," Emma said, trying to keep her tone respectful. "Do you have any advice on what I should do. I do not wish to allow my sister to starve or give her up… but I really can't afford to pay you back for my father's debt either."

"And nor should you," Gulliver said. He wrapped his arm around Emma's shoulder again. This time, there was no malice in the action. He drew her into him like some kindly uncle and began to walk with her back down the streets to the alley entrance. "I do not believe it is right that you and your sister should be lumbered with your father's debts, especially when you weren't even aware of the loans he was taking out to support himself here. So, here is what I am going to do…"

Gulliver paused. It seemed like the entire conversation had been leading up to this, and he was savouring the moment as he caught Emma up in his net. "You and your sister owe us nothing and my men will continue to look for your father to make him account for his debts. However, as you cannot afford to stay on in your home, I must insist that you work for me now."

"Work for you?" Emma paused in her tracks, unwilling to be led further by Gulliver as she felt unease rise in her. "Just what kind of work would we be talking about?"

"Not the kind you're worried about," Gulliver said, as though homing in perfectly on Emma's worst fears. "I keep several businesses in the city that always require new workers, people skilled and, more importantly, loyal."

Emma nodded. She wished she could feel relieved at Gulliver's assurances, but she could not. Something about the man left her certain he kept business in the most sordid lines of work. Still, if it meant keeping a roof over her head, Emma knew she would be happy to sacrifice a bit of her pride and standards.

"I'd be paid?" Emma asked.

"Yes," Gulliver affirmed. "No point keeping a roof over your head if I let you starve to death. If you work for me, I promise you and your sister will keep your home and get your meals each and every day. All this, and I promise the work will be nothing that taxes your morals or threatens your innocence."

Emma sucked in a breath. She hardly had time to think. Gulliver had begun to lead her again, pushing her toward the end of the alley and the main streets of London. In her arms, Mary was beginning to kick and fidget as she made her complaints and needs known once more.

"Very well… I'll work for you, sir, but only so long as I can see what it is that you'll have me doing, first."

"You're a prudent girl. I imagine you will not find yourself in the same hole your father did," Gulliver said, his words seeming to be complimentary. Digging into his pockets, he took out his wallet. Taking out eight shillings, the man grinned as he watched Emma eye them. "Enough money to keep you and your sister fed for the week. You get this now for coming out tonight and seeing the work I have planned for you. You'll get the same again each week providing you work hard and put in your best for me."

Emma felt a shudder pass through her as Gulliver pressed the coins into her free hand and then closed her fingers around them.

"I'll be working at night?" Emma asked, frowning.

"I suggest you see if some neighbour might be

willing to look after that child while you're out," Gulliver said. "Count it at as a blessing, you're more likely to find a neighbour at home and willing to watch the babe with the hours you'll be keeping."

Emma had no real response. The hours did not matter much: she needed the money. Still, knowing she would be working at night caused her mind to fill with those worse fears for the kind of work Gulliver had in mind for her. She guessed, well enough, it would be something that would test her morals, she just hoped it would not stretch them to breaking point.

CHAPTER 3

*E*mma rose from her bed swiftly and silently as she heard the call, careful not to wake her sister who lay next to her. It was almost impossible to hear the clanging of the dull bell over the onerous songs of drunkards and the ongoing dirge of an organ grinder that played in the streets just outside the free house, at the edge of the Rookery. Fortunately, the bell ringer was an enthusiastic fellow and rang for all his worth in competition with the city noise that never seemed to die away, regardless of the hour.

After checking that Mary was still sound asleep in the bed, Emma reached over to the small table and grabbed the old length of fabric she used to tie back her hair. The strip of cloth had once been a bright, rosy red colour, but use and dirt had rendered it closer to brown over time. The edges were frayed, but Emma hardly cared. She wound her hair back into a tight bun, taking care that not a single strand or lock was loose on her head. It was a most unattractive look to the once vibrant curls she used to wear. Emma pulled back her hair so tight it stretched her scalp, giving her the most severe look.

Wiggling out of her nightdress, she let the item fall to the floor as she moved to the old, slanted wardrobe. Opening the door and pushing aside the few dresses she kept for day wear, Emma bent down and retrieved the large wooden box that lay tucked in the back corner. Inside were dark, near-black trousers and stiff boots that rose above the knees. Both were several sizes too big for the slender woman, but they were not made for a woman either. Once dressed in the rather formless clothes, Emma put on her belt. She had to make alterations to it herself, adding a new notch far along the leather strap that best suited her petite waist. Experience had taught her to keep her clothes tied as close to her body as possible. She grabbed two lengths of rope and made a knot near the top of each stiff leather boot. She didn't want anything seeping in through a loose gap in her clothes; she didn't have the time to wash away the stink afterwards.

The bell rang again, Emma sighing in frustration at how little time she had to prepare. Pulling out a shapeless brown hat with a wide rim, she rushed to her door, not even bothering to pick up her nightclothes from the floor or put away the box she had taken from the wardrobe. She just grabbed the grey-white apron from the hangar by the door and stepped out into the streets.

In the dark, with her hair pulled back and dressed in such hideous clothes, Emma was a far cry from the country girl her father had once doted on. No men cast looks in her direction as she descended the stairs from the upper apartments of the Rookery and stepped over the bridge of detritus and muck onto the streets.

"You're late," the man with the bell said, arms crossed as he leaned in the shadow of the narrow passageway that separated the Rookery from London's more respectable streets. "If we miss the drop, I won't be coming here for you again, understand me."

"I'm sorry," Emma mumbled. She couldn't muster any real feeling behind her words. In truth, she would have been happy to never see the man or hear his dull bells from her window ever again.

Following behind the man as he led her out onto the lamp-lit streets and toward the Thames, Emma did her best to keep her head bowed and face obscured from all she passed. There was little danger from the shiftless drunks who wandered the darkened streets paying her a second glance, but she kept herself to the shadows all the same. She took no pride in what she did and wished no one to look her way as she went down to the river.

~

The waxen moon cast a soft silver light over the waters of the Thames. The tide was low, the sliver of reflected moonlight like a long winding ribbon to Emma's eyes. She stood on the mud bank with a dozen other shiftless souls, lined up like they were troops being sent into battle.

Three men—their commanding officers if they had been an army—inspected the line. One passed out lamps which they hung from rope cords about each person's neck. The second of Gulliver's men handed each man a long hoe. The final man had

EMMA'S FORLORN HOPE

nothing on him but held his hands clasped tightly behind his back, head held high and pompous.

"For the life of me, I don't know why I still fund this little venture of ours," the leader of the trio said. "These last weeks have been a poor showing from the lot of you and I am this close to folding it in and letting you find your coins elsewhere." For emphasis, the man pressed his thumb and index finger close enough together that they were practically touching. "Remember, if the law ever comes sniffing its nose to the sewer ways and finds what we are doing here, I am through. You rely on me to get you into the tunnels of the city, and I rely on you to make my risk worthwhile. I'm telling you now, if you lot don't start turning up treasure instead of trash, I'll be folding this business up, and I might even let the law know what you rats have been doing skulking around her majesty's sewers."

Emma kept her eyes on the river, hardly paying attention to her employers' threats. They were the same every time. No matter what she and the others dredged out from the sewers, it was never enough. They could bring back a ruby ring dropped from the hand of a duchess and the bosses would claim it was nothing. Conversely, she could come back with only a few pennies and bits of bent copper and her masters would not seriously think of shutting down their business.

"Toshers, you have three hours to prove your worth to us," the man continued as one of his fellows pried open the sewer grate with a crowbar. "You know the score, anyone not outside before sunup will be left inside to rot."

Emma turned and followed her fellows to the sewer grate, taking a last gasp of cleaner air before entering the stink of London's underground world. As she stepped into the dark, following the bobbing lights of the others, she tried to visualise her sister's face. She needed that image in her mind, the reason she was walking into such degradation.

~

For five years Emma had been at the job Gulliver had given her the day her father ran out on her. The old criminal had a good eye when it came to people. He knew exactly how far people would go to protect their family and earn a coin. He knew just how far into lawlessness and sin a person could be pushed before they dug in their heels. For Emma, work as a tosher was that limit.

The job was simple enough. All that was expected of a tosher was to scour the sewers beneath the city, wading through the muck and dirt in search of treasures that had fallen through the cracks from above. When she had first started at the odious and unenviable work, Emma had been surprised at just how much treasure was to be found in the sewers, how much money could be made with a sharp eye and a little effort. Coins, scraps of metal, even expensive silverware and pocket watches could be found amidst the sludge and effluence of the sewers. With a team of men and women combing different sections of London's sewers every night, Gulliver was kept flush enough to keep his affluent lifestyle while also supporting his workers.

Of course, it helped that the group of toshers he kept never got paid their full wage. When Gulliver had first given Emma eight shillings and promised her the same every week for hard work, he had neglected to say just how hard she would have to work in order to hit that bar. It was a mystery to her and the other toshers just how much treasure they were supposed to dredge up from the sewers each night to earn their 'full pay' but they had never once made that mark.

~

*L*amp on, head down, Emma moved with her group along the sidewalls and narrow platforms. Previous visits to the sewers by her team and others had left a network of wood beam bridges that allowed the toshers to safely cast their hooks into the muck and mire, or cross from corner to corner in the dark. They worked in lines, each clinging like limpets to the side walls as they fished through the slow-flowing mire for any treasures they sought.

Emma, to her great fortune, most often worked as a spotter. She had a sharp eye, even in the dark, which she attributed to years spent in the country where no streetlamps lined the roads at night. She would stand with eyes on the others, spotting out any suggestion of something unusual caught in the lamplight. The easiest treasures to find were those metal objects that still retained a shine. But most treasures were too covered in muck and effluent to glimmer in the lamplight. Five years had taught Emma to recognise their prizes by other means.

Blocking out the odours and stench, the grumblings of the newer toshers press-ganged into service, and the woozy, tired feeling that always threatened to close down her eyes, Emma concentrated on the line of sewage, pointing out suspicious shapes in the muck for her fellows to hook up. She was not above dipping her own hook and pole into the sewage, but Emma was sparing with it. Part of the reason she had lasted so long as a tosher, and not succumbed to sickness and disease, was the care she took in limiting her contact with the foul sludge she worked in, as much as possible. Others were not so careful. The newer toshers did not even bother tying their boots and trousers. Such foolhardy risk-takers usually learned their lesson after their first bout of sickness.

The timekeeper, another seasoned veteran of the sewer ways, brought Emma out of her careful study of the surface sewage when he noted they were entering their final hour of work. One of the greatest challenges of their work, beyond the obvious threats of drowning in filth or contracting illness from the sewer water, was how little time Emma and her crew were given to work. Though toshing had long been a career option for the truly desperate, Parliament had outlawed the practise almost a decade ago. Only people like Gulliver, unconcerned with the law and able to sneak down to the sewers at nights with a crowbar, continued the grim and disgusting work.

"How much have we taken?" the timekeeper asked. Emma could not see the old man's face in the dark, but she could easily hear the nervousness in his voice. He knew full well without a count that they had not taken in nearly enough to earn a word of praise from Gulliver. It was the kind of poor haul that would likely see their pay slashed to only five shillings if the next days followed a similar course.

"We need to spread out and get eyes on more areas," Emma said, skipping the man's question and moving to the greater issue.

"Agreed. Everyone will take a new direction and scoop up anything that looks solid. Don't be afraid to get your hands dirty."

Emma's nose wrinkled at the old man's rallying cry. Of course, she would do her utmost to ensure they left the sewers with their prize, but she did not relish the thought of getting her hands covered in more filth than usual in order to ensure she found the extra coins and scrap they needed to make their employer happy.

Moving deeper into the labyrinth of sewers, the light of the entryway disappeared as Emma rounded a corner. She began to probe with renewed desperation and fever through the muck about her. By now, her eyes were bloodshot and raw from so much close study in low light. She felt an earnest desire to rub her eyes, and it took all her will power to hold back. She did not need to get any of the filth she worked in onto her face.

Lips pursed, eyes narrowed, and hook stirring up the muck around her, Emma felt for anything solid that would put a few more shillings worth of treasure into their pot. She did not wish to go another week trying to survive on four shillings. She wanted just one week in the month where she didn't have to forgo a meal just so her sister could eat instead.

"Come on! Stop holding out on me!" Emma whispered in the dark. She was far gone caring about getting dirty. Every time she felt even the slightest resistance against her pole she reached in and grabbed whatever she could get. A coin rose up to the surface of the sludge, with what looked like a bent pewter mug and a few scraps of iron. Time was rapidly being eaten away and Emma knew she was pushing her luck.

The timekeeper hadn't given the final holler to warn them that they needed to get out, but she needed to be on the move before his signal came. She had wound up further in the sewer than the rest and it would take her longer to get back to the entrance. She was testing her luck. Gulliver never waited for toshers who stayed over their allotted time and ordered the sewer grate put back in its place even if a man or two was to be left stranded inside.

"Come on, just one more thing! Anything!" Emma hissed, spurring herself to find something good with her last stir of the fetid soup around her. To her surprise, something snagged on her pole. Just as the last of her hope ebbed from her, the pole stuck and Emma almost lost balance as she tried to force it to move. Not knowing what she had caught, but out of time to extract it carefully, Emma plunged her hands into the sludge, holding her nose as she reached deep into the sewage. Her hands wrapped around a cord, a metal chain of some kind. It felt fine in her hands and she groped around the thing to try and discover why it was caught. A rock or something had settled on top of the chain and Emma pushed it aside, biting her bottom lip as she tried to keep her hopes from rising too much. Still, it was hard not to.

Despite having spent years at the bottom rung of London society, Emma still knew fine jewellery when she felt it in her hands. The small links in the chain she had grabbed suggested a necklace and she swore she could feel a large circular pendant attached to it.

Finally, pulling her treasure from the dark black sludge, Emma heard the call from the timekeeper further back. She was already late in moving. She needed to turn tail and make for the sewer entrance at once, but she just couldn't bring herself too. Whatever she had in her hand, Emma had to see it, had to know exactly what it was. In the dark, the woman wiped desperately at the fine chain in her hand. She could tell at once that it was definitely some kind of necklace, and the pendant attached to it was unusually large and weighted. It was hard to wipe the muck from the thing when her hands and clothes were covered in sewage, but Emma managed to scrape off just enough to see a sparkle of red.

A gemstone?

"Emma, are you still up there?"

Emma flinched, clutching her prize tight in hand as the call of her fellow tosher frightened her. It was time to go. She knew beyond a shadow of a doubt that what she had found was an extraordinary find, its worth beyond anything the toshers had ever dredged up from the sewers before. In all her years working for Gulliver, Emma had never once contemplated cheating the man who kept a roof over her head... but this find was something else. Its worth had to be more than she could hope to make in a month from the miserly thug... enough to quit the city and return to the country even?

"Emma! The grates!"

The sound of her fellow toshers was receding rapidly. Though doubtless worried for her, none of them were going to risk their lives going back to see what had happened to her. Not a single one of them wanted to end up trapped in the sewers and it was every tosher for themselves when it came to getting out.

Emma moved. Risking safe footing for speed, she hurried down the sewer ways as fast as she could manage, nearly tripping into the liquid ooze several times as she struggled to keep to the narrow sides. Along the way, her boots caught on the tails of a number of rats, the hateful vermin squealing and lashing out with tooth and claw as she hurried down the passages to safety. A few of the worm-tailed fiends she batted away with her pole, clearing the path before her as best she could.

With some luck and fervent will to survive, Emma caught up to the others. She could just make out the shadow of one of them ahead of her and her mind relaxed in realisation that she would not be shut in the sewers after all. With that reassurance and confidence, another thought rose to the surface of her mind. Obeying that quiet voice inside without hesitation or question, Emma paused where she was. Holding the still stinking and filth covered pendant, Emma's face bunched up as she realised what she had to do. In all her years sloshing through the sewage beneath London she had never once sunk as low as this. She prayed her efforts and the risk that came with them would be rewarded.

Moving her hands to her trousers, Emma winced as she forced the treasure she had found inside. It was a poor hiding place, but she had to hope for the best. Gulliver's boys were hardly gentlemen, but they had never dared touch her anywhere untoward, even when patting her down after work. Her course set, Emma pushed forward again, rushing to catch up to the still retreating figures ahead of her.

CHAPTER 4

Ordinarily, the sight of the Thames and the lamps held by Gulliver's boys would spell safety and security for Emma. It meant she had escaped the sewers alive yet again. Tonight, however, her fears lingered even after she had made it through the grate and taken in a lungful of fresher, but still stinking, river air.

"You are all getting rather sloppy clearing out of the sewers in time," Gulliver said, his voice carrying that familiar note of disappointment in those who worked and risked themselves for him. "Do you know how much we risk lingering here so close to dawn?"

Emma caught her breath, eyes averted from

Gulliver as she tried to keep her calm during his usual tirade.

"I can only assume your delay in coming out means you found little of value for your dear employer this trip?"

No one dared make a reply to Gulliver, which was just how the man liked it. He seemed to take great pleasure in seeing his workforce beaten down, wanting them to feel worthless at the end of every night's toil. Emma had never quite been sure why Gulliver bothered. Each of them had spent the night wading through London's filth and were left stinking like latrines: just how, exactly, could they feel any lower?

Two of Gulliver's men came forward, one carrying a large cloth sack. Each tosher turned out the contents of their apron pockets, as was the custom, and then let themselves be patted down by the other. This was the moment of real danger and Emma held her breath as the two men drew closer to her. She tried to remain calm, assuring herself that she had stashed her find well enough, but the fear of being discovered remained with her. She had never once tried to cheat Gulliver, but she was pretty sure she knew what the penalty would be if she was caught.

"Boss, peelers coming!"

Emma looked up the bank of the river, where a lookout was leaning over the rails.

Gulliver cursed and instantly turned on his heels. "Rest of the booty in the bag and scarper! Everyone for themselves!"

It was a night of contradictions all over. On any other evening, Emma would have been terrified of being caught by a peeler. Toshing was still a crime and she would end up in the workhouse or worse if caught in the act. Still, on this night, her fear of Gulliver was greater than that of any bobby. Illegal though her trade was, Emma knew she would not be hung for the crime. Cheating Gulliver, on the other hand: that came with a host of punishments she would rather not know anything about.

Made to dump the contents of her apron hurriedly in the sack, Emma was knocked back by another of Gulliver's boys, the man already making a break for it as the last of the treasure was snatched out. Emma fell into the muddy, low tide of the Thames, cursing as she struggled to push up onto her feet. No one was going to help her. Gulliver had bolted before his men had even finished collecting up the treasure, and the other toshers were similarly scattering left and right, throwing down their poles as they looked to evade the law.

Emma slipped twice as she tried to find her feet. Her entire body was covered in mud now, and she could only scramble on all fours. Her eyes were wide with fear as she realised there was no hope of getting away before the bobbies came and peered over the embankment walls. She looked around her, finding only one safe hiding space.

The sewers.

Finger's digging deep into the mud to anchor herself, Emma pushed herself back to the sewer grate which Gulliver's boys had not yet closed up. The gate was heavy cast iron and Emma struggled to lift the thing as she slipped back into the tunnel ways. A miracle, or perhaps the strength of desperation, gave her just enough power to pull the thing loosely into place. She didn't have time to secure it, nor did she want to. Wading into filth, not caring how much of it oozed into her boots and clothes, she found the first corner and hid away in the dark.

For a time, all she could hear was her own heartbeat and heavy breathing in the dark. She listened as best she could to the other sounds, listening for the peelers who were almost certainly going to come and inspect the sewer grate. It took time, but eventually, she could hear voices.

"It looks like we had toshers here all right. You've got poles everywhere, boot prints going off every which way."

"Shouldn't we go after them?" a second voice asked, the voice young and uncertain.

"Could do, but not worth it. I don't want to have to go collaring anyone who spends their time skulking around the sewers. The smell is bad enough here at the entrance. You'd probably pass out and die just breathing too close to one of them sewer scum."

"So, we're just going to let them go?" The second voice carried a note of disappointment, and Emma could well imagine the man as a fresh, young bobby, eager to right the wrongs in the city and make his mark.

"You'll learn in time. There's enough crime in this city that you're never gonna collar them all. Toshers aren't the worst villains in London, and they tend to take care of themselves in the end."

"What do you mean by that?"

"Going into those sewers in the dark, wading through all that muck... Most toshers wind up killing themselves if they stay at it too long. Better to let them kill themselves in their vile business and

EMMA'S FORLORN HOPE

focus on those villains who are a real harm to others, eh?"

Emma remained silent. As she listened to the older bobby, she felt his message was in some strange way meant for her. As she held tight to the promising necklace she had pulled from the sewage, she knew she was right to take the thing. As the bobby had said, there really was no future in toshing. Gulliver had stacked the system so that she could never save enough money to take Mary and herself out of the misery and danger he kept her in. Sooner or later, the job would kill her. Whether by illness, drowning in the gruesome sludge, or something else entirely, Emma knew that every day she remained in the job was a gamble.

Biting her lip, Emma clutched the necklace in her hand tighter, her resolve redoubled. Taking the necklace for herself and attempting to run out on Gulliver was a gamble, but no worse than what she was already doing. Her father had escaped the villain's clutches five years ago, and Gulliver really had no reason to believe she'd betray him. In five years of service, Emma had never once put a toe out of line.

She would have to move fast, but Emma felt sure

she could make the escape she craved—the escape both her and her sister needed.

~

Once she was sure the bobbies were gone and the coast was clear, Emma moved to the sewer entrance. Reopening the grate was hard, and she marvelled at how much strength she had exerted in order to shut it up in the first place. Still, with a little work and a few well-placed kicks, Emma forced the grate open and staggered out onto the Thames embankment once again. The tide was beginning to come in, and Emma pushed down to the water's edge to try and clean off the worst of the filth and muck that covered her. The Thames was hardly clean itself. The waters were worlds apart from the freshwater streams and brooks Emma had known back in the countryside. Still, it would do the job well enough and make her sufficiently presentable for the journey home. Of course, any observant bobby might want to ask her why she was soaking wet, but Emma was sure she could come up with some excuse. Besides, as dawn threatened to creep upon the world, the clouded sky threatened rain. With any luck, the heavens themselves would provide the excuse she needed.

Clinging to a fragile hope, Emma moved along the water's edge, careful not to wade too deep into the river and get caught in its powerful current. The water was freezing against her skin as she let it rush over her clothes and body, driving away the worst of the sewage that clung to her. She worked meticulously and fast, wringing out her hair and splashing her face several times until she was quite soaked. As she worked, the cloudy skies overhead loosened their blessings upon the city, a sudden and fierce downpour of rain that would more than adequately serve her on her journey home.

Wet, dishevelled and tired beyond reason, Emma still wore an inordinate smile as she rushed down the cobbled streets and narrow thoroughfares in the direction of home. A few peelers crossed her path, but they stood under shop doorways and covered alcoves. None looked keen to stop her in her tracks and Emma made it back to the Rookery without having to trade a word with anyone. She climbed the rickety stairs to her small, one-room apartment, chest heaving from exertion. She only held back and took stock when she was at the door.

Mary would not understand what was happening. In her bid to protect her younger sister's innocence, Emma had never told Mary what she did to put food on the table, nor spoke of the sinister and threatening man who controlled their lives. As far as Mary was concerned, Emma worked in a factory during the night. She would ask questions if she saw the necklace and would never understand why they had to leave so suddenly and quietly. Emma could only hope her sweet and innocent sister would be so enthralled by the possibility of a trip that it simply wouldn't occur to her to ask questions at all.

"Emma!"

Even as the door was halfway open, Mary was scrabbling onto her feet and running to the door to meet her. She threw her arms out wide to hug her older sister, but Emma nimbly dodged out the way. Despite the impromptu wash she had taken in the river and the rain, she did not want her younger sister touching her after a night of scrambling through the sewers.

"Emma, where were you? Did the factory make you stay late?" Mary stood in place. Her nose wrinkled up a little, perhaps smelling the lingering stench on her older sister. "What's that smell?"

"No questions now, Mary," Emma said, marching into the apartment and throwing open the wardrobe doors. Immediately, Emma started to bundle up their best clothes and anything of importance they might need on a trip. One dress she put aside; the rest wrapped up in a bedsheet.

"Emma, what's happening?" Mary asked again.

"We've… We've got a chance at a new job," Emma said, making her story up as she went.

"You're leaving the factory? No more late nights?"

"Yes, Mary, no more late nights. But we must hurry. This job opportunity… it won't be there for long and we need to move if we're going to have a chance of snatching it up. So, do you think you can be a good girl, and do exactly as I say?"

"Yes! Yes, Emma, I will be the best girl ever!" Mary's enthusiasm brought a smile to her older sister's lips. It was both a relief and validation of her actions to see how Mary leapt at the opportunity for a fresh start.

"Finish packing our things away, while I get changed," Emma ordered, grabbing the clean dress she'd put aside. Getting out of her toshing gear was a struggle, and foul odours released into the air with each layer peeled off. Emma ignored the curious glances Mary gave her as she changed, washing her feet and arms with a fresh jug of water before slipping into her day clothes. She also used just a little of the water to clean off the prize she had found in the sewer.

It was hard to keep the thing from Mary's view. Emma had to move right into the corner of the room, hunching over the bowl of water as she gently caressed the object with her fingers. Slowly, gold link chains and a dazzling ruby the size of a man's eyeball revealed itself. Its worth was incalculable, and Emma bit her lip as she considered all the possibilities the treasure would open up for her once sold.

It was before nine when the girls were dressed and ready to leave. The last thing Emma did was to shutter the windows and pull away the hidden floorboard where she'd kept the minuscule savings that she'd managed to pull together over five years of labour with Gulliver. With the gold and ruby pendant wrapped in a handkerchief and pocketed deep in her dress, Emma took her sister's hands and put their small, sad, one-room apartment behind them.

CHAPTER 5

Emma's first course of action was to wash herself properly, buy new clothes, and reinvent her image. If she was to successfully sell the fine piece of jewellery she had found in the sewers, she would need to make herself more presentable. In her tired, worn dress, with her body reeking of sewage and dirt, there was no way she could sell the thing without someone suspecting her of having stolen it. She would need to clean up her image and present herself as a comely servant, a maid to a household perhaps.

Eager to hide as far from Gulliver's sights as possible, Emma spent the morning pushing through the city, taking a room at an inn far away from the pokey little apartment she had kept. She ordered a room for herself and her sister, along with a bath. The later was a rare joy for her. Or, rather, having someone draw her a bath and have the time to fully and studiously clean herself, was a rarity. The water that filled the copper tub in the upper rooms of the inn was filled with warm water. It was not quite a hot bath, but it was certainly better than the cold-water baths Emma was used to. Were it not for the need to keep on with her plans, Emma would have taken the time to enjoy the comfort and indulgence she had paid for. Instead, she worked hard and studiously to clean herself.

Emma felt ashamed as she scrubbed and sponged at her skin. She had thought herself quite clean for a tosher, but only once she began to truly look to the business of cleaning herself did, she realise how much grime and muck had settled on her and never left. It was under her nails, it was in her hair, and it had left a grey film upon her skin which she had never fully noticed until now. As the tub she sat in grew steadily darker, Emma felt no small amount of embarrassment as she had to call in the maid and ask for the tub to be refilled. The maid was similarly aghast and gave Emma a wide berth. She did not even bother to remove the dark grey water in the

EMMA'S FORLORN HOPE

tub, merely brought in their only other bath from the other room and set it down next to the first.

Two baths were enough to see Emma restored to a perfect picture of health and beauty. When she wiped away the steam from the mirror and looked at herself, she was amazed at the transformation she saw. The embarrassment at how dirty she had been dissolved as she realised how beautiful she could be. It was hard to describe, but the simple act of bathing left her feeling like she had restored something of herself that was lost. It was as if the physical sponging of her skin had also expunged all the darkness and trials she had endured under Gulliver and now emerged reborn into a new world and life.

Of course, enchanted though she was with her new look, Emma did not have the luxury of time to indulge in the view. Instead, she threw on her clean clothes as fast she could, not even waiting for her hair to fully dry before she left the inn. Emma did not feel good about leaving Mary in a strange inn all alone, but she did not wish to risk anything happening to her sister should any of Gulliver's men spy her out on the streets.

With her newfound pendant cleaned and wrapped in her best kerchief, Emma stepped out into London in search of a buyer for the thing. She could not try the regular markets; no baker or trader she knew had the money to buy such an extravagant work of art, nor would they wish to. There were certain dealers Emma had come to know through her association with Gulliver and his men, but she did not dare go to them. Though they would have happily bought up the necklace without asking questions, Emma knew that word of the sale would reach Gulliver's ears. So, she did the only thing she could think of…

Hawking.

Moving into the finer West End of London, hoping her cleanly appearance would give her an air of respectability, Emma began knocking on doors, showing her newfound treasure to any who would take the time to look. When asked by housekeepers and servants just who she was, Emma introduced herself as a maidservant in the employ of a Mrs Albridge. It took a few doors for Emma to perfect her story and cover, but she soon had it down to a tee.

Mrs Albridge was a respectable and wealthy woman who was hoping to surprise her husband, with a luxurious present for his birthday. However, not wishing to dip into their funds too far or let on to her husband as to her plans, the clever Mrs

Albridge had sent Emma out to sell some items of jewellery she no longer cared to wear in order to fund her plans.

It was a ruse that worked well enough. The servants at the doors made no attempt to check Emma's story and seemed sufficiently pleased in her look not to assume her a common thief or worse. Still, for all this, Emma could not find a single lady who would take the time to look at the small treasure she was looking to sell.

At each house it was the same story. Whether she talked to a servant or the lady of the house, Emma was told to take her necklace elsewhere. The affluent and men and women of the streets she walked down did not take kindly to hawkers and would not buy jewellery from a woman they did not know.

For over an hour, Emma walked the pavements of the fashionable end of London, knocking on doors and praying that each new door would be the right one. Though everyone she encountered treated her with sufficient politeness, it was still hard to maintain her enthusiasm for her endeavour as she moved to another black door on the end of another row of well-to-do houses. As she knocked on the door, Emma was even beginning to wonder if she should perhaps return to Gulliver. If she took the pendant with her and handed it over willingly, he might not question why she had not tossed it in the bag with the rest of the loot that morning. Who knew, he might even reward her…

The door opened and Emma banished her defeatist thoughts from her head as she prepared her speech once again.

"Ah, are you a maidservant?"

Emma stammered, surprised to have the man before her asking questions before she even had a chance to speak. She frowned a little and studied the man. It was clear whoever she was dealing with was no servant. His black suit was too pristine, the collar of his shirt too crisp-white and well pressed. The watch dangling from his waistcoat pocket was in silver by the look, as were his cuffs.

"I am, yes," Emma said, curtseying politely. It was the first time in her rounds she had been met by the man of the house and she almost wondered if she should make her excuses and leave. Her astute eyes noticed no ring on the man's finger and could only assume he had no wife to gift a necklace too. Then again, perhaps he would have a suitor? As Emma looked to the man, she thought it more than likely he would have a woman of some sort desiring his attention. He had handsome features, warm brown eyes and short dark hair that was just a little untamed. Emma had a hard time believing such a man was without female admirers.

"Well, come on in. I am glad to have someone call at last."

The man's words were odd indeed, but Emma did not think twice at following him into his home. It was the first time she had been let inside by anyone, and she wondered if perhaps the man was starved of company, given his odd statement.

"Can I offer you anything to drink, Miss…?"

"Morton, Emma Morton." Emma did not look to use her real surname. "And… I would not wish to trouble you."

"Really, it is no trouble at all," the man said with a smile. "I had just about given up on anyone calling today and I am thrilled you are here. I had not long put some tea on to brew in the pot and would be happy to make you a cup, or a coffee, while we talk. In fact, I insist upon it."

"Well, that is very kind of you, Mr…?"

"Mr Barton." The man said his last name with a raised brow. "I take it you did not study my advertisement in full?"

"Advertisement?" Emma bit her bottom lip, brow knotting in growing confusion as she found the man before her harder and harder to understand.

"Yes. You are here for the housekeeper position, are you not?"

"Housekeeper position? Yes, of course." The words came from Emma's lips before she had time to check herself or consider precisely what she was doing. It was a moment of impulse and blind instinct that drove her, just as strong and powerful as the one that pushed her to take the necklace from the sewers for herself.

"Your accent… it doesn't sound like you are from London?" Mr Barton seemed to have an excellent ear.

"It is true, I am from the country, sir," Emma said, her mind whirring fast to reshape the cover story she had invented for herself. "I was housekeeper to a lovely woman called Mrs Albridge, who sadly died a few months ago. She was staying in London at the time of her death. Her family informed me my services were sadly no longer required after my mistress's death, so I decided to remain in the city where there was more chance of finding work for myself."

"I see…" Mr Barton said, a slight grimace on his

face. "I am sorry for the loss of your mistress. Were you close to Mrs Albridge?"

"Quite close, yes," Emma lied, taking a seat and smiling at the man as he began to pour tea from a freshly made pot into two china cups. "Mrs Albridge was a very kind woman, as fine and fair a mistress as one could ask for."

"It is a shame her family could not keep you on in their employ. Do you mind me asking if there was any particular reason her relatives decided not to keep you on?"

Mr Barton's questions were challenging, and Emma once again had to think on her feet, wondering just why she had pretended to be answering his advertisement.

"Mrs Albridge was quite old and frail. Her younger relatives are already well established and comfortable in their own homes and lives and simply didn't have a need for me," Emma said. "I bear them no ill will for the decision."

Barton nodded, laying down a cup of tea on the side table next to Emma's chair. As he moved over to his own seat, Emma took a glancing look around. It was the first time she had bothered to take in Mr Barton's home. It was a somewhat spartan affair for a monied man. There was little in the way of art adorning the walls, just a long bookcase dominating the western wall. The fireplace, on the east side of the room, lit the room in a cosy orange glow, but the grate and hearth were in need of a clean. Barton's chairs were plush and soft, but not exactly ostentatious. Either he was not as well off as Emma had first assumed, or he was very frugal in his spending habits.

"I will be frank, Miss Morton, I have been in need of a decent housekeeper for some time now. I am a busy man and haven't the time to find a wife who'd put up with me and care for the home."

"I am both sorry and surprised to hear that," Emma replied, blushing a little. "I would have thought a well to do man such as yourself would have little trouble finding a wife willing to keep you… Though, I am obviously glad no one has, otherwise this job opportunity might not have arisen." Emma's blush deepened as she feared she was rambling. To her relief, Mr Barton laughed at her comments.

"Well, you are most kind. I suppose, if I were to take the time to go courting around London, I might find a woman who would settle for me, but I have been told by friends I am far too serious and involved in my work."

"And just what work might that be?" Emma asked, settling into her chair a little as the conversation became ever more natural and pleasing.

"I am a lawyer," Mr Barton said, taking a sip of his tea. "I work with several important clients with businesses in London. I hope this will not sound too much of a boast, but I never would have been able to afford a residence like this when I first came to London as a humble secretary for a firm. I have had to work hard to reach my place and position in life and it has left little time for frivolities such as courtship and romance."

"I don't think it a boast," Emma assured. "You should be rightly proud of what you have accomplished here." She felt an immediate liking to the man opposite her, a smile remaining on her lips as a not uncomfortable silence came between them.

"I suppose, in light of Mrs Albridge's death, you would not be able to provide a reference for me?" Mr Barton brought matters back to business and Emma sucked in a breath as she realised the hurdles still before her.

"I am afraid not. Though getting on in years, my mistress never much considered what would happen to me on her passing, and I had put little thought to it either. I should have wished her heirs to write me a reference, but as they saw very little of their mother in the years I attended her, there is not much of any meaning they could write by way of a reference."

"I see." Mr Barton didn't seem entirely pleased with Emma's answer, but he was not sending her away either. He took a deep breath and took another sip of tea as he considered things.

In the silence, Emma studied the man closer. There was something handsome about him, an intensity behind his sharp blue eyes that suggested a supreme wit and intellect. Those eyes flickered to her often as he considered his course and Emma found herself curiously eager for the man's approval. His eyes on her were somehow thrilling and a girlish part of her hoped he would see something in her, even if taking a job in his home was not at all practical. Emma did not know what the man was looking for in his chanced glances toward her, but she hoped he would find it all the same.

"Truth be told, I have been too long without a housekeeper to be picky, and you are the only one to have answered my advertisement. I am happy to take you on and see how well you keep the place. You might find I have occasional need for your help in my offices too. While I try my hardest, I have a terrible tendency to leave my files and papers in a mess."

"I would be happy to fulfil any needs you have of me," Emma said, scarcely believing where this bizarre conversation had led. She felt the necklace in her pocket, biting her lip a little as she tried to discern what her next step should be. She had trusted her instincts to guide her while speaking to Mr Barton, but she truly had no idea why she had decided to play the part of a housekeeper answering his advertisement.

"Am I to take it you have no residence in the city to call your own? I should prefer it if you would take the servants room here," Mr Barton said.

"That would suit me very well... although..." Emma hesitated, biting her lip a little as she considered the one fly in the ointment.

"Is there some issue?"

"Well, I should mention I have a younger sister in my care. She is only five years old and my responsibility. Mrs Albridge was very understanding of my desire to care for my sister myself rather than leave her in the care of others. I should perhaps have mentioned it sooner, but would you be willing to... I know it would be a dreadful inconvenience..." Emma's words died with each word she spoke, and she stared into her teacup with a most morose expression on her face.

Barton smiled. "I can understand your loyalty to your sister, Miss Morton. As it happens, I have two servants' rooms in this house that are vacant and am happy to give both to you and your sister. So long as she will not interrupt my work or make a nuisance of herself during my meetings with clients, I am happy to keep her here."

"Oh, she is very well-behaved, sir. I promise she will never stir from her room or cause you a bother, ever."

"Well, let's not be too draconian," Barton said with a wry smile. "I hardly wish to keep your sister a prisoner in an attic room. She may wander the house as she pleases during the day. I only ask she keep to her room when visitors are attending and out of my office while I work."

"I am sure you'll find her as good as gold and better," Emma said with a smile.

CHAPTER 6

Without even meaning to, Emma had found herself as a housekeeper to a respectable lawyer, a roof over her head, and the kind of comfortable accommodations and furnishings she had not known since the old farm. If she had known how easy it would be to land a position in a good home with a few choice lies, she would never have accepted Gulliver's offer of work all those years ago. Then again, Emma suspected her appointment to Mr Barton's home was yet another stroke of good luck. It certainly helped that her new employer was content to believe her stories and lies without asking too many questions.

Mary settled instantly to their new home. Emma's little sister relished having a bedroom of her very own and, despite assurances that she did not have to stay there, seemed perfectly content to spend hours at a time enjoying the space that was hers and no one else's.

Mr Barton himself was patient and kind. It certainly helped matters that he had never hired a housekeeper before in his life. Emma suspected the man had only vague ideas of what to expect from her, and this certainly played to her advantage as she tried to fulfil the role she had so unexpectedly landed. Not that she tried to abuse the man's trust and generosity. Though never having intended to become a housekeeper, she wanted to do her best for the man for as long as she was with him—but that was another matter altogether. How long was she planning to stay under his employ?

When Emma had accepted the position of housekeeper, she let instinct and desperation guide her. It became obvious she would not be able to sell the valuable jewelled necklace she had taken from the sewers in a single day. She needed the position at Mr Barton's home while she worked to find the right buyer for the prize. In her off-duty hours, she continued to ply the streets, knocking on doors in the hope of finding someone who would buy her necklace. The fresh, new uniform Mr Barton had bought her certainly helped add to her credibility and a few times she was even admitted into homes to show off the jewel she hoped to sell. But still, she had not found a buyer.

Through it all, though, Mr Barton's home offered a safe haven and protection. Emma suspected Gulliver and his boys would be looking for her by now. The villain never liked to let anyone out from under his crushing thumb, and he would surely know Emma would never run from him unless she had money to escape. He would be looking for her, but Emma felt certain the man would not dream of her hiding out in the home of a respected lawyer. Gulliver would be looking for her in the inns, enquiring at factories, and searching the other rookeries in the city. So long as she kept to the finer centres of London, sold the necklace soon, and planned her escape carefully, Emma felt sure she would be able to complete her plan and quit London for good.

"You seem suitably distracted there, is something on your mind?"

Emma blinked, remembering where she was and flushing with embarrassment as her employer's gentle words reminded her that she should be dusting down the shelves. Emma had no idea how long she'd been stood on the footstool, staring off at the window as she again poured over her plans and charted her course.

"My apologies, Mr Barton, I was just... Just lost in thought for a moment."

Barton's cool blue eyes lingered on Emma as she stood there on the small step ladder, a slight smile forming on his lips. This was not the first time he had caught her stood in thought and the sight never seemed to fail to bring a smile to his lips. Emma wondered if the man mistook her odd silences for evidence of some deeper thoughts below the surface. He seemed the philosophical type, and Emma had often found herself watching him in turn as he mused over private thoughts in his office or the sitting room chair.

His eyes, at last, moved away from Emma, as he walked into the living room. He took his usual seat by the fire and seemed to put effort into staring at the well-tended flames, almost as though he were forcing himself not to look back at her. Emma moved off of the footstool to attend to him. "Might I make you something to drink, sir? I can come back to the cleaning in here later if you'd rather not be disturbed."

"Thank you, a cup of tea while I look over these

notes would be most appreciated," Barton said with a gracious nod.

Emma curtseyed and turned to leave, pausing as her master's voice called after her. "I hope whatever is troubling you will resolve itself soon, Miss Morton. If you need it, I am happy to offer council or a listening ear."

Emma sighed as she walked off towards the kitchen to make the tea. She knew Mr Barton was only trying to be kind to her, but his kindnesses only made her ashamed. Soon enough, once she had successfully sold the necklace she kept hidden away from sight, she would look to quit his home silently and without warning. It pained her to think of abusing the man's generosity and kindness so. At these odd occasions, when he seemed to treat her as more than a servant, it was all the harder.

Banishing the guilty thoughts that stirred in her mind, Emma tried to focus on making the tea, ears twitching as she thought she heard a light scurrying sound from the hall. Shaking her head, Emma continued with her work, filling the milk jug and sugar bowl as she let the tea brew in the pot. She had struggled to carry the silver tray in her first days in Mr Barton's house, frequently spilling milk and hot water on the tray if she moved too fast or didn't look where she was going. She moved carefully and methodically down the narrow hall passage, taking care not to brush against the umbrella stand near the staircase. As she went, the sound of conversation caught her attention. It was coming from the sitting room. Mr Barton was talking animatedly to someone, though Emma had not heard any knock on the door. She listened for a moment, her body going stiff as a familiar girlish laugh followed the man's muttered words.

"Mary?"

Emma picked up her pace, rushing into the room and quickly setting the tray of tea down on the side table. Mary was kneeling by Mr Barton's chair, her head resting on the arm of the plush seat as she looked up at the man.

"Mary! What have you been told about the rules!" Emma scolded, immediately moving to pick up her sister and extricate her from the room before Mr Barton could complain.

"Oh no, it is quite all right, Miss Morton," Barton assured. He waved a hand for Emma to cease her fussing. "I caught sight of an inquisitive little head peering in at me from the hall and thought it was high time we had a proper introduction."

EMMA'S FORLORN HOPE

"Mr Barton was telling me about Africa," Mary said, a huge grin on her face.

Emma gave a stiff, awkward smile. Though pleased to find her sister had not caused any offence or trouble for her master, she did not like the thought of Mary lingering long in Barton's company. She had told Mary that they needed to pretend their name was Morton, and to not tell their employer anything about their past, but she did not know if Mary could be trusted. She was only five and prone to forgetting rules and instructions when excited. One wrong word and Mary could yet spoil it all for them.

"Miss Morton, why don't you make tea for all of us," Barton suggested. "I'm far happier talking awhile rather than looking over these musty case notes, anyway."

"Of course, sir," Emma said with polite courtesy. As she moved over to the tea tray and began serving, she listened carefully to her sister behind her. The slightest hiccup or word out of place and she would need to find some way to intervene.

"Did you see any lions in Africa? Or Elephants? Did you ride an elephant, Mr Barton?"

"I did, and do you know what?"

"What?"

"I was the most scared I have ever been in my entire life. I was only a little older than you when my father took me to Africa and the elephants seemed taller to me than the tallest houses in London."

"I wouldn't be scared of an elephant," Mary said, her voice definite as she puffed out her chest.

"I am sure you wouldn't," Mr Barton agreed.

Handing her employer his tea, Emma found herself making another cup for herself as well as cutting three slices of fruit cake for them all to enjoy. Mary, on Mr Barton's insistence, was given the biggest slice of all. This pleased Emma on so many levels. On the one hand, it was nice to see how generous and good her employer was with Mary. But, better than that, the cake also kept Mary's mouth busy and ensured she couldn't let anything slip that she was not supposed to.

What should have been a brief cup of tea and an amicable conversation between employer and servant quickly turned to three hours of Mary forcing Mr Barton to recite his life story and adventures. It turned out he had quite the interesting life. His father was a steward to a noble family and, consequently, travelled frequently with his master to holdings in India and Africa. By the time he returned to England, apprenticed to a law firm in London, he had seen much of the world and had stories aplenty for Mary to delight in. After a time, Mary began to fall into a doze. She sat near the fireside, her upper torso and head leaning on a footstool as the fire warmed her into slumber. Emma smiled to see her sister so contented and worn out.

As the comfortable silence deepened, Emma found her gaze moving from her sister back to Mr Barton once more. He was a handsome man to look upon. That was a fact Emma could not deny, even from their first meeting. Still, the more she came to know the man, the more his handsome qualities seemed to be accentuated by the goodness inside of him. Emma had not known anyone who would take the time to indulge Mary for so long in stories, and she felt a warm thrill inside of her as she watched the man so easily handle her excitable younger sister.

Across the room, Emma could hardly pretend she did not notice Barton's eyes falling on her from time to time. She did not know if it was wishful thinking, but she felt as though the man's eyes lingered on her a great deal in these quiet moments. She would not ever have called her master out on it. Even forgetting the impertinence of it, Emma had to admit to herself that she enjoyed the man's stolen glances in her direction. Spending the best years of her young adulthood dredging through London's sewers had not allowed Emma to catch the eye of any kind of suitor and the looks she sometimes garnered from her employer sent the warmest of feelings through her even as they coloured her cheeks in embarrassment.

"I hope you will forgive my impertinence," Mr Barton said, his voice a whisper in the quiet room.

Emma was so lost in her study of the handsome lawyer sat opposite her she almost didn't realise he had spoken at first.

"Your impertinence? I would have thought I should be apologising to you," Emma said, with a faint laugh. "It was very generous of you to indulge my sister as you did, but I am quite sure she has stolen away your entire day. She will do so again if you are not careful," Emma warned.

"I was happy to be so diverted. It is nice to find someone so eager to listen to my stories from the continent."

"Has no one cared to listen before?" Emma asked. "I must confess, Mary wasn't the only one to be enraptured by all you've seen. You are lucky, very lucky indeed, you were able to see such things."

"I was, indeed… but I do not have much chance

or opportunity to speak of those days. Self-made men such as I can find acceptance in London's upper echelons, but those folks do not care to be reminded of where you have come from. They would rather not hear about the grubby little steward's son running around the streets of India with friends he had made in the market stalls."

"I see. Well, more is the pity for them," Emma said, with a reassuring smile. Mr Barton smiled back, his chest swelling with pride. Emma watched as his eyes moved back to Mary. She could not explain it, but she could almost feel the man's warm regard for her younger sister—for them both, even.

"I hope you will not think this an impertinent question, Miss Morton, but what is Mary's education?"

"It is not as good as it could have been," Emma answered, trying to remain vague and diplomatic in her answer. "Mrs Albridge required much of my time and attention and I have not had the funds to see to a tutor for Mary. She has attended Sunday school of course and can write a little, though she has never had much chance to practice."

"Would it… Would it be overstepping my bounds if I offered to sponsor your sister's education, perhaps hiring a tutor who could teach her?"

"A tutor?" Emma felt her jaw go slack and she struggled to find the words for Barton's generous offer. "I... I would, of course, be so grateful and pleased... but I couldn't possibly accept. The wages you are already paying and the roof over our heads... Why would you even wish to give so generous a gift to us?"

Barton's smile seemed to wane a little, his look becoming melancholic and sad as he stared at Mary. "Once upon a time, Miss Morton, I had a sister. She was born while my family were in India."

"Really, you never spoke of her in your stories?" Emma said, her voice hesitant as she feared she was treading a path best left undisturbed.

"She died in the cholera epidemic," Barton said. It was a short answer, filled with emotion. Emma knew it would be a cruelty to force the man to give details and listened attentively, a sympathetic look upon her face. "Your sister has a similar spirit and curiosity to my dear Elizabeth. She always had so many questions and would even sit at the foot of father's chair, just as Mary did today."

"I am sorry if my sister stirred up unhappy memories for you. It must have been hard to speak of those days in India with her, as you did."

"I won't deny a few of the stories were attended

by some feelings of melancholy, but I mostly found the experience quite cathartic."

Emma nodded, sucking in a breath as she tried to think of what to say. That sad look was still very much in evidence on her employer's face and she wanted to do something to help alleviate the darker thoughts that seemed to be brooding within him. Standing from her chair, she moved across the room and put a hand on his shoulder as he sat there. It was a most presumptuous move for a servant, but Emma felt confident the man would not reject the offered comfort.

"I am exceedingly fortunate to have found my way to your home, Mr Barton," Emma said. "I hope you will not think it presumptuous of me to say this, but I am sure your sister would be very proud of the man her older brother has become."

Barton was silent for a moment as he moved to take Emma's hand from his shoulder. He placed his hand on hers, the two standing in silence for a moment while Mary slept blissfully unaware by the fire. A strangely familial feeling washed over Emma at that moment, a feeling of home that she had not known since her Mother had died. In that instant, the idea that her days in Mr Barton's home would not last seemed most unfair.

"Are you certain you wish to trouble yourself with my sister's education?" Emma asked. She bit her lip after speaking. She shouldn't be asking the question at all. As soon as she found a buyer for the necklace she should be looking to steal out of London and start anew in the country. Still, something had shifted in her that afternoon. Reckless though it was, impossible even, Emma felt a sudden and deep desire to stay by Barton's side. Working as a housekeeper in another man's home was the last thing that she expected for herself, but it was fast becoming the place she wanted to be. To see Mary sleeping so soundly by the fire, she knew her sister felt the same.

Mr Barton took his time answering the question. It did not seem as though he was unsure of himself, but rather giving due diligence before answering. "I will not press the matter if it would make you at all uncomfortable. Still, I would want to do this for you both. Your presence, both of you, has been most welcome in my home. After so long pottering around all alone in the house, dedicated only to my work, it is pleasing to have life around me again. I want to do what I can for you both, to thank you for that spark of joy you have brought to the place."

"As I said before, I am quite sure the wage and the

roof you put over our heads is more than sufficient for Mary and myself. I certainly wouldn't wish to impose on your kindness. However, if you are truly willing to bring in a tutor for my sister, then I would be more than grateful. It would be a gift neither of us could ever hope to repay you for."

"Then it is settled," Mr Barton said, looking up at Emma and smiling. "I shall make enquiries in the week and see what comes. Hopefully, I will find a tutor faster than I found myself a housekeeper."

CHAPTER 7

*E*mma lingered near her sister's room on the upper floors. She knew she should be downstairs, starting the dinner before the hour became outrageously late, but she simply could not tear herself away. Through the thin walls, she could hear Mary as she struggled through her lessons. Her sister was not the most adept of pupils, but what she lacked in innate ability she more than made up for in perseverance and stamina. As soon as Emma had told her that Mr Barton was paying for a tutor for her, Mary had made all kinds of promises of how good she would be and how proud Mr Barton would be when she learned to read and write as he did. Listening to her painfully slow progress being made in the next room, Emma imagined it would be a long while before Mary reached that point, but it pleased her beyond words to see her sister growing, blossoming as Mr Barton's generosity and patronage opened new doors for her.

"How is she doing in there?"

Emma gasped, putting a hand to her chest as she wheeled around and found Mr Barton stood right behind her. He was so close that their bodies were nearly touching, and Emma found herself involuntarily biting her bottom lip as she watched the man draw back a step.

"I am sorry, I didn't mean to frighten you," Barton whispered again, an amused smile on his lips as he studied Emma's face. She was quite sure her cheeks had turned beet red and she lowered her gaze in embarrassment as she tried to find her words.

"I… I should have been paying more attention. Come to think of it, I shouldn't even be up here, eavesdropping on my sister."

"You have heard no complaints from me, Miss Morton. Trust me, if I am ever dissatisfied with your work, I will be sure to tell you. For now, I am happy to indulge you while you eavesdrop on Mary. So, how is she doing?"

Emma turned back to the door, feeling a warmth on her back as Mr Barton drew in closer. He was not quite touching her, but she could still feel his presence. It was a heady and distracting feeling, and Emma almost couldn't concentrate on the sounds coming from the other room at all. Instead, her ears attuned to the sound of Barton's breathing behind her, the slight rustle of his clothes as he moved.

"What is she doing in there? I can't quite make it out?" Barton's whisper in Emma's ear sent a shudder straight through her and, moment by moment, she swore her sanity was leaving her, replaced by some new sensation that she both craved and sought to quash all at once.

"... I think... I think the tutor is trying to have her read from some children's fairy tales... I must admire the tutor for their patience. I do not think Mary has yet made it through even a whole page."

"She has great resilience," Barton whispered. "I had feared, once the novelty of learning had worn off, she might not care to be taught anything at all; but I am told she keeps at her studies no matter what setbacks come before her."

"She gets that tenacity from our mother," Emma said, freezing up when she realised that she was perhaps speaking a little too unguardedly of her past. She straightened up, bumping into Barton awkwardly as she tried to move away from the door.

In that instant, she nearly tripped. The distracting power Barton held over her seemed to overpower even her basic ability to look where she was going, and Emma gasped as the man caught her up in his arms.

Another silence passed between them. These had become common in the last days. They stood, seemingly frozen in time, as Emma looked to her master and he back at her. She could feel his strong hands on her back where she had been caught. Barton's fingers seemed almost to caress her for a second and she thought she detected his lips moving closer to hers. At the last, though, sanity and common decency reared its head and Barton drew back, his usually proud and confident gaze suddenly falling elsewhere.

"I... I should get back to making the dinner," Emma said, pushing past Barton and moving to the stairwell. It was hard to describe her feelings in that instant. The sensation of her master's touch as he had caught her, that feeling of his lips moving to hers. She could not decide if those things were real or a figment of her own desires. Could her master really have any care or desire for her?

And what if he did? As Emma retreated down the stairs, she tried to remind herself once more that she could not allow herself to become too settled. Barton did not even know her real name. If his attentions toward her were more than imaginings, Emma knew she should work to dismiss them. She had no right to the man's heart—she was not worthy of his consideration for all the lies she had fed him about her past.

As Emma fled down to the kitchen, she resolved not to let such a moment pass between them again. And, even as she made that promise, another part of her knew she would be incapable of keeping it.

CHAPTER 8

"What are you doing?" It was a question Emma found herself asking several times a day as the weeks in Mr Barton's service began to spill into months. As she watched Mary settle into a routine with her tutor and became more comfortable and content in Mr Barton's company and presence herself, Emma found she was looking for excuses not to go out with the necklace in her spare hours. With each passing day she became bolder as she walked the streets of the West End. When she looked in the mirror and studied herself, she wondered if Gulliver's men would recognise her now, even if they were to pass her in the streets. Free of the grime, dirt and trappings of her old life, Emma felt she had metamorphosed into an entirely different creature from Emma Moss. Emma Morton looked respectable, clean, above-board. No back-alley thief or fence would look at Emma Morton and believe she ever could have roots in London's shadier quarters, nor slept in one of the pokey back alley rookeries. She began to think that she might remain in London in safety without a need to flee to the countryside.

As she stepped out of the house with a wicker basket held underarm, Emma wore a smile as she set off down the streets. She puffed out her chest, standing tall and proud as she moved alongside the other denizens of London. She smiled to passers-by and exchanged greetings with servants from other households she had begun to recognize on her outings. Her steps were confident, and she no longer sought to keep her head bowed in concealment except when forced to areas in the city she knew well from her old life.

Moving down an alleyway that gave servants quicker access to the markets, Emma paused in her step as she noticed a group of men lingering in a corner. There were four of them, and Emma knew on instinct that they were up to no good. From her days as a tosher, Emma knew a guilty look when she saw it. The men in the alley did not linger casually.

EMMA'S FORLORN HOPE

Their bodies were tense and their eyes roamed outwards, looking at the few passers-by with suspicious glances. If Emma had to guess, the men were scoping out the back alleys, looking for ways into the nearby homes. Emma knew Gulliver kept operations in the city even less clandestine than toshing and she could not help but wonder if the men she saw were under his thumb. It was the first time she had seen their type so close to Mr Barton's home and the sight brought her old fears immediately back to the forefront of her mind.

Sucking in a breath and turning her head to look sharply away from the men, Emma continued on her way to the market, resolving not to give another glance back. Whoever the men were, she needed to stay out of their way, leaving them to their shady work with the hope that they forgot all about her.

As she moved back out onto the main streets Emma again resisted the urge to look behind her. Despite the noise of the city all around, her sharp ears and intuition told her she was being followed. Rather than let her potential pursuer know she was on to him, Emma resolved to continue on her way. She picked up her pace a little, hoping to lose whoever stalked her in the more crowded marketplaces. Whatever she did, Emma resolved not to return back to Barton's home until she was quite sure she was no longer being pursued. The last thing she needed was for one of Gulliver's men to track her to her home. Even if her pursuer did not recognise her, she did not wish Barton's home to be brought to her old employer's attention for any reason.

The city markets were busy, but not busy enough for Emma to shake the entity that followed her. Though she had not once looked back to see who was stalking her, she could tell she was still being closely followed. It did not matter where she moved or how big the crowd, always the feeling remained with her until she began to suspect her mind was playing tricks on her. Her fears of Gulliver surely were fuelling some paranoia in her and Emma stopped. She was now far from where she should be and had wasted a good hour of her time. The idea that she was fleeing from some imaginary phantom brought her, at last, to turn about and look behind her to see just what, if anything, was the cause of her fears.

Never in her life had Emma paid more dearly for indulging her curiosity. As she turned around and looked to the sea of faces behind her, she found her eyes locking with another. The figure stood about twenty paces back from her, his form half-hidden behind a cart. He seemed to comprehend that he had been spotted and came out of the shadows, removing the shabby, formless hat from his head.

Even at twenty paces, even after five years, Emma recognised the man who stared back at her. She recognised his lazy slouch, his watery weak eyes that darted to avoid her even as he ambled toward her at a slow shuffle. Emma stood her ground, hands balling into fists, as she watched the man that she had never thought to see again approaching her.

"It is you, isn't it, Emma?" Thomas said. His voice was a shaky whisper as he came to a stop a few paces from her. Emma stood a little taller, chin raised as she looked down on the man she had once called her father.

"I hadn't expected to see you back in London again after you abandoned us," Emma said, not wishing to waste time in idle chit chat. She barely wanted to hear the man at all, except there were questions she wanted to have answered. "Gulliver has been looking for you for years now. I promised him I'd tell him if ever you tried to contact me. You still owe that man a debt."

"I know… In fact, that is why I am back in the city," Thomas admitted. He ran his hand along the back of his neck as he used to do whenever he was forced to admit to his errors and mistakes. "I came back to London hoping to find you and Mary but ended up running into Gulliver's men instead. Seems no amount of time is enough for those boys to forget a face."

"You're... You're running with Gulliver again?" Emma felt a chill run through her. Suddenly, thoughts of confronting her father on his crimes against herself and Mary were banished from her mind. The idea that her father was back in Gulliver's pocket and could rat her out made her eager to leave at once. "I... I have to leave. I don't want to hear any of this. I don't need your excuses as to why you left us, or even an apology. Just leave me be."

"No, wait, Emma!"

As Emma tried to get away, her father reached out with grasping hands, anchoring her in place as he looked at her with eyes that seemed wild, almost hungry. "You've done well for yourself... Gulliver wouldn't tell me what had become of you when I was dragged before him by his goons. All he said was that you had quit his home one night and never returned."

"And? Let go of me! I don't want to talk to you."

"You're doing well for yourself now. You must

have money, to be dressed like that… You could help me. If you could square my debt away with Gulliver, I could come back… I could be there for Mary. Surely, she still needs to know her father? It will be like the old days! We could—"

"Get away from me!" Emma yelled, struggling against her father and swatting at the scrawny but powerful hands that held her in a feral grip. When that didn't work, she began to scream.

"Help! Police! Police! This man is trying to rob me! Help!"

Emma did not know if any peelers were near, but the threat alone was enough to force her father to let go of her. His brow knotted in confusion, surprise, and resentment, settling on his weathered and tired features as his own daughter tried to hand him over to the police. That look turned angry, but Thomas was not able to do anything against her now. Too many eyes had turned to look on them and several men were stepping forward to interpose themselves between Thomas and her.

"Please, that's my daughter! This is a misunderstanding, she's just a little upset," Thomas pleaded with the two men advancing on him. His voice still held that grovelling quality that could make anyone feel for him. The two men looked back at Emma and she just shook her head.

"I don't know who this man is or what he wants! Please, get him away from me this instant." Emma knew the words of a frightened woman outweighed those of a dirty vagrant and she sighed in relief as the men turned on her father once more. Thomas seemed to know he was out of options. He turned on his heels and ran. Emma didn't know if she was relieved or disappointed to find that the men who had come to her aid were not prepared to chase after him.

～

*E*mma returned home without even buying the items needed from the markets. She rushed through the streets, lifting her skirts and pushing through the crowds with tears in her eyes as she made for the safety and security of Mr Barton's home. She did not even consider how she appeared when she charged through the front door and feverishly locked and bolted it shut behind her. Her chest heaved with exertion and her vision was blurred by tears. As she heard an uncertain call from Mr Barton's office, Emma sank to her knees on the floor. She tucked her knees up and wrapped her arms around them, rocking herself gently, head low so her employer could not see her face.

Even as she sobbed, Emma could hear the stirrings in the house. Mr Barton came out of his office and immediately gasped to see her on the floor, empty basket thrown to the side.

"Good heavens, Miss Morton, what on earth happened? Are you all right?"

Emma had found her tears coming harder as the kind gentleman bent down next to her, putting a consoling arm about her and pulling her into a protective embrace. Barton remained ever good and noble in everything he did, and Emma hated to think about what would happen if ever he learned the truth of her past.

"Emma? Emma!" A second voice, shrill and frightened came from the top of the stairs and Emma looked up to find her sister charging down the steps toward her. Mary threw herself at her older sister, wrapping her small arms around Emma's neck and crying even though she did not know what for.

Looking up to the tutor on the stairs, Barton sucked in a breath and sought to restore some sense of order. "Please, I know you are here to teach, but could you possibly go out into the kitchen and make us some tea, Miss Morton here is in some distress."

"No… No, it's my job… I don't want to be any trouble," Emma said, struggling to her feet as she tried to pull herself together. Neither Mary nor Barton were letting her get away though.

"Miss Morton, I will not hear of it. You are clearly in need. Now, please come through to the sitting room and tell me exactly what happened. Did someone attack you on the streets? Do I need to call for the constabulary?"

Emma couldn't answer. She could only shake her head lamely as she was pushed in the direction of the sitting room. Despite the fears, upset and pain tearing through her, a part of her knew she needed to find herself and quickly. She could not let Mr Barton or Mary know the truth of what happened but needed a lie that would be convincing to them both.

"I… A man in the streets tried to rob me… Some men came to assist me… he didn't get away with anything from me… but… but…"

Emma's lip quivered as she felt Mr Barton's strong arm about her, his hand massaging her shoulder soothingly as he led her to a chair. "Whether they took anything or not, I am sure that must have been quite the ordeal, Miss Morton. I will call for a member of the constabulary to come at once. Can you remember what the man who accosted you looked like? Whereabouts in the city were you when this happened?"

Emma's head hurt as she listened to Mr Barton's urgent questions, each one forcing another lie upon her to remember and keep track of. She did not know if she could endure it. It came as a relief when the man left the room to rush out onto the streets. He was doubtless running to find an officer of the law. Emma took deep breaths and just clutched Mary to her.

"It will be all right, Mary," Emma found herself whispering. "It will be all right, I promise. I won't let anything happen to you."

CHAPTER 9

For three days, Emma jumped every time there was a knock at the front door. She found herself lingering near the windows at all hours, looking out on the streets for any figure of character who might be lurking near their door. She never once saw anyone who looked remotely suspicious, never saw her father's wiry silhouette shifting about, but Emma could not shake the suspicion that the house was being watched and that shadows from her past were circling ever closer, like hungry foxes cornering a hapless rabbit.

Mr Barton's assurances and offers of comfort were of no help. All his words did now was reinforce in Emma how much of a fraud she was, how great a deception she had played on the man who had let her into his home. If the truth about her past ever came out, how would she be able to look him in the eyes again? After letting him pay for lessons for Mary, it felt like her continued presence in his home was an affront to the man, a further insult she was paying him. And yet, Emma could not leave. She knew beyond a shadow of a doubt there was danger waiting for her on the streets. If she tried to leave Mr Barton's house now, tried to sell the necklace and make off into the night, she was sure someone would catch her.

Emma's grim feelings of foreboding rose to a head exactly five days after the meeting in the market. She was working in the kitchen, trying to keep her mind focussed on her work, when a loud rap at the door caught her attention. It was the rap of something metal on the door, a cane handle perhaps. As Emma approached the door, a second impatient rap was heard, and she jumped a little as she put out a nervous hand to unlock the door and admit the caller.

Opening the door, a fraction, Emma's eyes widened as the familiar, portly form of a man she recognised came into view. Still holding his silver-handled cane like a club, the man looked even more evil and intimidating than ever as his eyes locked with hers. Emma's breath caught in her throat and she whispered the name on her lips.

"Gulliver…"

All at once, Emma tried to slam shut the door, throwing her weight against it hard. Gulliver was too fast. Using his cane like a crowbar, the man stopped Emma from shutting up the door, and Emma could not resist as strong hands on the other side of the door forced the thing open. Emma screamed as two peelers rushed into the house, each with a baton raised. She ran to the stairs, blindly hoping to get to Mary, but was caught by one of the two bobbies who held her in a painful hold. He pushed her against the wall, Emma flinching in pain as her cheek connected with the door frame of the sitting room.

"What is the meaning of this? Who are you?" Mr Barton emerged from his study and rushed at once to the door. He put a hand on the bobby holding her, immediately pulling him off and forcing him back toward the door. Emma did not know her master possessed such strength, but she doubted he could save her now.

"I demand to know what is going on here!" Barton ordered, standing in front of Emma protectively.

EMMA'S FORLORN HOPE

Emma looked to Gulliver, the portly old villain scowling at her as the two bobbies flanked him on either side.

"We've received word from this gentleman that the woman presently cowering behind you is a known thief and has stolen something of great value to this man."

"That is absurd," Barton replied, not wavering for a moment.

"Is it now? Tell me then, how it is that I have heard of my wife's necklace being offered for sale to all the fine folk living in the vicinity of your home, sir?" Gulliver said, his voice laced with a sense of righteousness that Emma knew was false.

Emma felt all hope drop like a rock in water. How had Gulliver found out about the necklace? She did not know how the man had discovered her secret but felt stupid for having underestimated the man's cunning.

"Necklace? What necklace what are you on about?" Barton gave a backwards glance to Emma.

"Sir, this gentleman believes your maidservant may have stolen his wife's ruby necklace some time ago and has been trying to sell it while working in your home," one of the officers said, his voice a measured calm. You're a lawyer, are you not? That's what the plaque says outside your home?"

"I am," Barton replied cautiously.

"Well, then, you will know it is best in these matters to comply with us as we investigate the matter. A quick search of your servant's room and belongings should quickly settle this matter, don't you agree."

Emma shuddered as the only one standing between her and Gulliver lowered his guard. "Very well, officers. You may search the house if you wish, but I insist that neither of you lay a hand on my servant in the meantime. I will not have this woman, who I have the utmost faith in, treated like a criminal in my own home."

Gulliver seemed to smile at Emma, almost relishing Barton's impassioned speech in her defence.

"Might I ask you to wait outside, sir," Barton asked Gulliver, nodding toward the door. "The law requires that I make myself and my home available to the constabulary, but I do not have to afford you such."

Gulliver turned on his heels and shrugged his shoulders. "As you wish. I am sure it must be distressing to think that you have let a thief and villain into your home. I am sure I will be accepting your apology before long."

Emma watched as Gulliver stepped out onto the streets. She could already hear a clamouring upstairs, Mary calling for her as her tutor kept her locked in her room. Emma knew there was no hope for her. She had not even hidden the necklace well amongst her things. A look in the wardrobe and a rummage through her clothes and the peelers would have her. She looked to Barton; her eyes wide with fear. He stared back, seeming to understand her gaze.

"Miss Morton… is any of this true? Please tell me this is all a lie and you have not been using my home as some… some base to use while you hawk stolen wares to my neighbours.

"Mr Barton… I… I…" Emma could not find her words, and before she could find the right thing to say a call echoed from up the stairs.

"We have it! We have the necklace!"

Emma felt her whole body go rigid and then limp. She slumped down onto the stairs, her eyes glazing over as she listened to the sound of the officers pushing back down the stairs to arrest her. The whole while, Mr Barton stared at her, eyes wide with disbelief. She watched as he took several steps back from her, already wanting to distance himself from her. As the peelers made it to the bottom of the stairs, Emma put up no resistance as they pulled her to her feet and marched her out of the house. Mr Barton did nothing to stop them. He just stood dumbfounded and wounded. Emma tried not to meet his hurt gaze or Gulliver's smug smile as she was led outside to a waiting cart. She obediently sat down as the door was closed behind her and locked. Quietly, she began to pray for Mary, prayed that Mr Barton would not throw her sister onto the streets or give her up to a poor house. Emma had failed her sister, failed the promise she had made to her mother to protect her. Now, her only hope lay in Mr Barton's kindness and grace. Emma found it hard to imagine that even he would be willing to continue looking after Mary after the deception she had played upon him.

CHAPTER 10

Gulliver had worked hard to seize hold of Emma. When brought to the jail and read her crimes, Emma began to get an idea of just how the tenacious villain had discovered her and how he had come to learn of the necklace she held.

Her own father must have told Gulliver of his meeting with her and this had surely piqued the man's interest. Gulliver was not the sort of man to give up any asset he felt he owned, and Emma was sure Gulliver saw her as his property.

Discovering the necklace took more shrewd cunning from the conniving thug. He must have realised Emma would not have left her home in the Rookery unless she had found something valuable enough to make a new start elsewhere. By the sound of things, Gulliver had sent his little spies out onto the streets near Mr Barton's home: his eyes and ears quickly learning of the housekeeper who had recently taken work in the area and had been seen going between houses from time to time with a necklace of considerable value. After learning all he could of Emma's movements and dealings, it was the simplest thing for Gulliver to report a robbery and frame her for theft of a precious ruby necklace. The villain had been sly enough to get the peelers to do his dirty work for him and now Emma found herself in jail, no doubt facing the hangman's noose if Gulliver was to have his way.

The jail was overcrowded with miscreants awaiting trial. Emma found herself thrown in with fifteen other women who all eyed her finer servant's clothes with curiosity and envy. A few seemed downright malicious and Emma tried to keep herself to the corners and shadows as she waited for her fate to be revealed to her.

As she lay cold and frightened in her cell, Emma wondered just who would come for her in the end. She half expected Gulliver to request to see her. She could imagine the man coming to gloat at his victory over her, perhaps paying the guards to look the other way as he dished out some extra punishment for having had the gall to cross him. Despite the threat Gulliver posed to her, Emma found her fears centring more on her sister than herself. With no way of knowing where Mary was or what Mr Barton would have done with her after her arrest, Emma could only fear the worst. If Mary had been sent to the workhouse, or thrown out onto the streets, then Emma would have failed in the promise she had made to her mother—failed in her duty as a sister.

~

*E*mma was not sure, but she estimated that three days had passed by the time she was brought to trial. Her body had grown stiff from the cold and lack of use during her wait, most of her time spent huddled on the floor of her cell and trying to escape the pain of her situation through sleep. She wore the same dress she had worn on her arrest, the fabric shabby and stained from overuse. As she was placed in chains for her journey to the courts, she looked at her hands. They were grubby and reminded her of the old days. Gulliver had clawed her right back to her starting point, reducing her to ruin and a misery worse than she had known in the small attic room in the back alley. When she considered the pain she had caused Mr Barton, and the danger she had put her sister in, Emma wished she could take all her work of the last months back. She felt foolish for having ever tried to raise herself higher than Gulliver allowed. Better to have worked the sewers, obedient and true, until she died. That was what Emma told herself as she was led to her sentencing.

~

The courthouse was small and cramped. The petty court had only a few benches for observers at the back of the court, a stand for the accused, and the judge's seat. As Emma stepped inside the courtroom, she immediately caught sight of Gulliver. She thought the man would be pleased to see her there in irons. She thought the villain would relish the sight of her bowed and broken by his hand. Instead, the man she saw before her was not the Gulliver Emma knew. He paced the court floor, his eyes darting nervously about, with beads of sweat on his brow which he mopped with a dirty kerchief. Emma knew that look well, but never on her old master. Those agitated movements and fretful expressions were exactly those of her father, whenever he had been caught out.

Emma looked to the judge, sat bored and tired in his seat. The man looked like he had endured too many trials already that day, sat slouched, and drumming his fingers as he waited for his latest case to begin. The stands were empty but for one soul, someone Emma had not expected to see at all. Her eyes widened and her mouth fell open as she caught sight of the flowing golden locks.

"Emma!"

Mary shouted at once, running forward with tears in her eyes. Emma froze in place, pushed forward by the officers leading her inside. Another officer in the court moved to stop Mary from rushing to her sister's side and Emma felt a knot in her stomach to find her sister present to witness her downfall. Was this some further insult by Gulliver? Had the man prevailed upon Mr Barton to surrender Mary to him, perhaps using Thomas to gain control of the one treasure Emma had left? Emma could well believe Gulliver capable of such a thing, but that strangely nervous look on Gulliver's face suggested something else was out of place.

Emma stepped into the court, offering a nervous

smile to her sister as she was placed in the dock. She looked around, uncertainly, still trying to divine what in this whole situation had Gulliver so nervous.

"We are gathered to hear the case of Mr George Thornton versus Miss Emma Moss. The defendant stands accused of theft of a gold and ruby necklace belonging to Mr Thornton's wife," the clerk said. "Defending Miss Emma Moss is Mr Nicholas Barton, who will be here presently."

Emma's eyes widened and she turned to look at Gulliver, now going by the name of George Thornton. Suddenly, Emma understood why the man was nervous. It likely had never occurred to the villain to think that Mr Barton would look to take the trouble to defend Emma at trial. Emma had no idea what power had persuaded her employer to come to her aide, but hope began to grow in her heart again as a side door opened and Mr Barton strode into the room.

The man was resplendent in his black robes and cap. He walked with authority and purpose toward the docks, papers in his hand and a determined look on his face. Emma felt a stirring in her spirit, imagining the man to be a knight of legends come to her rescue and she bit her lip in anxious anticipation.

EMMA'S FORLORN HOPE

"Let Mr Thornton present his case to the court," the judge said. Compared to Emma and Gulliver, the judge showed no interest at all in the affairs before him. Emma looked to Gulliver as he tentatively approached the stand. She wondered if his real name was George Thornton, as the court knew him, or whether this was but another pseudonym he adopted when required.

"My Lord, the facts of this case are clear and plain," Gulliver began, not quite summoning his usual deep tenor to his voice. "Two months ago, my home was robbed and a valuable necklace, gold with a ruby pendant, was stolen. Word of the necklace surfaced about a month later when I received word of a woman posing as a housemaid going around the doors of the West End, trying to hawk such a necklace to any who would take it. After some patient investigation, I traced the thief to the home of that man, Mr Nicholas Barton, and called upon the aid of the law to recover what was mine. The officers who attended the scene did find my necklace at the property of Mr Barton, thereby proving this woman's guilt... I do not think the case can be put any more succinctly and plainly than that, and I am surprised that Mr Barton has been allowed to defend the accused here today. As her master, I would say that the man is too involved in the case and should not be allowed in the court at all."

"Well, if the facts of the case are as plain and clean-cut as you surmise them to be, then I would think you would have no objection to my defending Miss Moss today."

"The matter of Mr Barton's representation of the accused was already agreed upon before the trial began and I am in no mood to rake over matters already discussed," the judge answered, quashing Gulliver's hopes of silencing the lawyer. "Mr Barton, if you have some evidence to exonerate your housekeeper, let us hear it immediately."

"Thank you, your honour."

Gulliver was forced to take a seat and Emma noticed the way he began to eye the side exit nearest him as Barton prepared to speak.

"Your honour, I will not attempt to disguise the fact that a grave deception was put upon me by this woman. Emma Moss came to my home under the guise of Emma Morton, inventing for herself a life story that was entirely false and untrue. I took her into my home in all good faith, I even arranged for her sister Mary to receive lessons at my expense."

Emma bowed her head in shame at Barton's words. She did not know what to expect when he took to the floor to speak, but his opening words stung deep.

"I will admit that a deception was played upon me, but it was a deception played in desperation and by necessity, rather than by malice. Thanks to the honesty of Miss Moss' younger sister to me after the arrest, and a chance visitation that illuminated the full truth of matters to me, I am now able to reveal to the court, the true nature of things." Mr Barton took a deep breath, looking toward Gulliver with righteous indignation that made even the thuggish ogre of a man squirm in his seat.

"Miss Moss was brought to London five years ago and conned into a contract as good as slavery under this man, Mr Thornton. She and others unfortunate enough to fall into his web were made to scour the sewers of London at night, forced to wade through the muck and mire for any worthwhile objects or coins that could be found there. Mr Thornton here, who I believe also goes by the alias of Gulliver, kept these workers in poverty and misery, using threats and extortion to keep them from speaking out against him. Miss Moss tried to escape that life after finding a most exquisite and miraculous find in the sewers, a necklace of gold and ruby such as the one Mr Thornton described to the court. Wishing to escape her life under this tyrant's thumb, she fled with the thing, hoping to sell it in order to gain enough money to escape the city. Is this not so, Miss Moss."

"It's… It is true. I never meant to hurt or injure you when I came to your home that day. I was just —" Mr Barton raised a hand, indicating that Emma should be silent.

"This is a most fanciful tale," the judge said. He had sat up a little, his interest in the case seeming to pique as Barton laid his case. "I assume, Mr Barton, you have sufficient evidence to support these outlandish claims."

"I do, Your Honour," Barton assured with a nod. "When Mr Thornton here came to my home to arrest Miss Moss, I do not think he ever expected me to keep her younger sister, Mary Moss, in my care. Fortunately, for all involved in this case, I did not have the heart to punish an innocent five-year-old for crimes another had committed. My natural instinct was to press for custody of Mary Moss within the courts."

A slight smile etched over Emma's face to hear of Barton's goodness to her sister. It was a relief beyond all others to know that the man had not cast

Mary out or held her to account for all that had happened.

"Mary was of great assistance in helping me come to the bottom of this case, revealing the truth of her living conditions and what little she knew of her sister's work and life before coming to my home. However, this alone was not enough to convince me that Emma Moss was not a thief. It was Mr Thornton himself who provided the vital piece of evidence I needed in order to learn the true nature of things." Emma glanced to Gulliver, who sat with arms folded tight about his chest, head still turned to the door.

"Two days after Miss Moss' arrest, I was surprised to receive a visitor claiming to be Miss Mary Moss' father. The man seemed most eager to gain custody of his child, but I was amazed and curious as to the man's remarkably good timing in coming in search of his daughter. I brought the man, Thomas Moss, into my home and pressed upon him to reveal the truth of his visit and how he knew just where to find his daughters and why he should come so suddenly for Mary." Barton paused and looked to Gulliver with a look of triumph on his face. "You should know, it did not take your lackey long to betray you, Mr Thornton. When you create an empire based on greed and manipulation it should come as no surprise when your pawns turn on you. All I had to do was offer Mr Moss money enough to clear his debts to you and he happily explained all to me about your enterprises and how Emma had come to be trapped within your web." Turning once more to address the judge, Mr Barton straightened his robes. "Your honour, I have had Mr Moss kept in the adjoining room as a matter of prudence. I did not wish for Mr Thornton to be spooked and have a chance to escape when he saw one of his own come to testify against him."

Emma looked to Gulliver. The entire court looked with her. It wouldn't even take her father's testimony to reveal the man's guilt. Gulliver already looked ill and feverish in his seat. Before the side room door could even be opened to admit Thomas Moss into the court, Gulliver bolted. Rushing from his chair, he ran to the nearest door screaming obscenities and curses as two officers tackled him and restrained him by the arms.

"I hope, Your Honour, you can see the guilt in this man's eyes? If my testimony and the testimony of Thomas Moss, still to be heard, were not true, why should this man look to flee as he is?"

Emma breathed a sigh of relief. Though the trial

was not yet over, Gulliver's actions were tantamount to a confession. As her own father slunk into the room, like the worm he was, she braced herself for his testimony and account. She knew though that her freedom had been assured, that Mr Barton had freed her from Gulliver forever, perhaps saving countless other lives in the process.

CHAPTER 11

Outside the courtroom, Emma was reunited with her sister. She bent down on her knees and scooped Mary into her arms, sighing in relief as she stroked the girl's golden curls and kissed her cheek. However, it was not a perfect family reunion. Even as she hugged Mary tight to her, Emma noticed her father shifting toward her, a tentative look in his eyes.

"Well, we managed to get justice against old Gulliver at last, eh?" Thomas said, shifting his weight back and forth as he stood before his two girls. "I never thought I'd see the day, but I am glad I could help in taking that man down."

"Yes, it must feel very good to have accepted

money from my employer in payment for coming forward with the truth."

"Emma, I—"

Emma raised her hand, cutting off her father before he could try and worm his way back into their lives.

"Please, do not try and insult my intelligence or degrade yourself further by pretending anything you did here today was out of a desire to protect myself or Mary. You only agreed to testify against Gulliver when another man offered you more than Gulliver could. I'd be very interested to know just what you were planning to do with Mary when you first called at Mr Barton's home for her."

Thomas ran his hand over the back of his neck as he shrugged his shoulders. "Gulliver had asked me to get a hold of her to make sure Mary didn't say anything she shouldn't to Mr Barton. Gulliver did not know how much your sister knew of your old life and was nervous when Mr Barton did not immediately give her up."

"So, you can admit your aim was to sell us out again, to give Mary over to Gulliver so he could enslave her the way he did me? And after all that you still have the gall to suggest you helped bring Gulliver to justice."

"You're not my father," Mary said, her innocent words adding to Emma's as both girls' stood against him.

"I know what you're trying to do, Thomas," Emma said, not even deigning to call him father anymore. "Now that you are free of Gulliver, you want us back so I can work and bring in money to support you as you drift through life as you always have. Well, it is not happening. You have the money Mr Barton paid you to come forward with the truth. I suggest you just take it and go. Don't waste your breath trying to worm your way back into our lives. Save what little dignity you have left."

Emma knew her father had no real care or interest in her or her sister, but it still hurt to see it so plainly displayed. Once Thomas could see there was no way he could charm his way back into her life and pocket he just turned around on the spot, dug his hands into his pockets and wandered away without so much as a backwards glance. Emma hugged Mary tighter in her arms as she watched the man leave. "Don't worry, Mary, we don't need him."

"No, we have Mr Barton," Mary agreed. Those words hurt Emma more than her father's leaving them ever could. While her master had come to their aid when they needed him most, Emma wondered if he would wish them to remain in his home. He seemed genuinely upset in court at the deception she had played upon him and, as he came over, Emma braced herself for the worst.

"Well, Miss Moss, you are a free woman. While it is not my business to interfere in family matters, I believe you made a very good choice by turning away your father back there. He does not deserve you—either of you."

"Thank you, sir, ... And thank you for everything you have done for me. Truly, when I woke up this morning I expected to be sent to the gallows."

"There is no need to thank me," Mr Barton said with a slight smile. "In truth, I was hurt to learn the reality of your past, to learn how you had deceived me. However, I more than understand why you had to lie. Your story is... well, it surprised me, Miss Moss, and, once I got past the deception you played on me, I will confess I found myself admiring you all the more for all you have done and endured."

"Admiring me?" Emma was stunned by the man's response, a slight blush colouring her cheek as she repeated his words.

"You have worked so hard for your sister. Working in the sewers for five years, daring to stand up to a fiend who ruled over you, and other unfortunate souls, like some tyrannical king."

"I am relieved you think so. In all that I have done to protect my sister these past years, lying to you and abusing your generosity was the only thing that caused me guilt or shame. I wish I had just trusted you with the truth from the start. I should have trusted you with it but..."

"You could not have known how I would react back then," Mr Barton said. "However, I believe the time has come to discuss reparations."

"Reparations?" Emma asked, her brow knotting in confusion.

"Well, I am an eminent city lawyer and my services in court do not come cheap. Along with the money I used to gain your father's testimony, I am afraid I must insist you repay me for my troubles."

"But sir... you know I have no money. I couldn't possibly—"

"You will return home with me, at once, and continue on as my housekeeper at full pay. Your sister will continue to take lessons, and I will not hear one cross word about it. Am I understood?"

Emma could hardly believe her ears. A broad grin crossed over her face, and Mary's as well, at their employer's continued generosity, despite everything that had passed between them.

"I promise I will work harder than ever to ensure that I repay you for all you have done for me," Emma swore. "I will keep the house so clean you will never encounter another mote of dust in your life."

Mr Barton laughed. "Well, I look forward to that; though I will be happy enough to have my tea delivered without any being spilt on the tray." Emma blushed again at his teasing jibe. "Well, then, shall we go home?"

CHAPTER 12

FOUR MONTHS LATER...

*E*mma stood outside her sister's door, biting her bottom lip and trying to remain as quiet as possible as she listened to the sounds coming from within. Mary truly had Mr Barton wrapped around her finger and it pleased Emma greatly every time he gave in to her wishes and climbed the stairs to tell her stories of his adventures in Africa before she retired to bed. Mary hijacked so much of the man's time; Emma marvelled that Barton ever had time to put to his work. Still, he never once complained.

As the noise in the room died away, Emma stepped away from the door. Mr Barton smiled as he exited the room, careful to close the door quietly behind him. Emma smiled back at him as they moved to the stairs, going down to the bottom floor together before either dared to speak.

"You know, she will never grow tired of your stories no matter how many times you tell them to her," Emma chided playfully.

"Then it is a very good thing I never seem to grow tired of telling her my tales… though, I will admit I may have begun embellishing certain truths of late to make the tales more interesting."

"You mean to say you didn't singlehandedly fight off an entire pirate galleon that threatened the ship that took you and your father to India."

"Not singlehandedly, no," Barton said with a smirk. "Care for some tea? I'll make it."

Emma shook her head, her smile remaining on her lips. "You must be one of the worst master's in history. Do you even understand what it is to have a servant? I am quite sure our roles have been crossed somewhere along the way."

"Just let me do this for you, Emma," Barton said. His use of her first name surprised her and Emma felt a slight thrill inside as he gestured to the sitting room. "If you'll go through, I have something waiting for you on the mantlepiece… a gift of sorts."

"A gift?" Emma watched as Mr Barton moved away to the kitchen without another word. Intrigued by his curious actions, she stepped into the sitting room, freezing in place as she caught sight of her 'gift'.

Delicate gold links wound like a snake's body about a brilliant, blood-red stone. There on the mantle was a necklace, the necklace Emma had found in the sewers so long ago now and which she had thought would be her gateway to a better life. She stood frozen in place; mouth agape as she tried to process what she was seeing. When Mr Barton's voice came as a whisper from behind her, she jumped in fright.

"The tea is brewing," he said, as he moved into the room toward the necklace. "I trust you like your gift."

"I… how did you even…"

"Well, after Gulliver was arrested and his assets taken, the necklace you found in the sewers became the subject of some interest for me. For a time, the constabulary insisted that we look for its rightful owner, but when no one came forth to claim it, the jewel was put up for auction. I… I felt a strong desire to buy it, to return it to its rightful owner." As he spoke, Barton undid the clasp of the necklace and moved behind Emma. She could feel him press against her back just a little as he slipped the necklace about her neck, the ruby and gold chain looking out of place against her servant's clothes.

"This is too much... How much did you even have to pay for this?" Emma asked turning on the spot and looking at Barton with wide eyes.

"A gentleman never boasts on how much he has spent on a lady," Mr Barton replied with a smile. His look then became a shade more serious. "This gift, however, is more than a simple present, Miss Moss. I must confess, I bought it with another intention in mind."

"You did?" Emma asked, her voice a nervous whisper as their bodies lingered close together. Her breath caught in her throat as Barton's hands wound with hers.

"I know a ring is the traditional way a man is meant to do this, but I felt the necklace that brought us together to be a more fitting gift and token of my feelings."

Emma gasped, tears beginning to pool at the edges of her eyes as she watched her master move down onto one knee before her.

"Miss Emma Moss. Even before I learned the truth of your past, I admired you and found myself developing certain feelings for you. Now, knowing who you truly are, my regard and admiration have blossomed into feelings I can no longer control or deny. If you would accept, I would ask you to complete my happiness by consenting to be my wife, so that I might continue to spend the rest of my days attending to your happiness and the happiness of your sister. If you will let me, I want to fill the remainder of your days with all the joy and light that should have been yours all along."

Emma bit her lip and reached out with a hand. She rested her palm against Barton's cheek, sighing as his lips kissed her there. Moving onto her knees with him, Emma threw her arms about him. Holding tight to the man who had twice already saved her life.

"I could never ask for a better man or husband," Emma whispered in his ear, kissing his cheek as she felt his strong hands move through her hair. "The day I found this necklace, I thought it was my ticket to a better life, but it was never the necklace. It was you. It was your goodness and grace that saved myself and my sister. You have made me so happy since I met you, and I will dedicate my every day to making you as happy as I can, in turn."

The couple kissed, holding each other on the floor as the fire crackled quietly in the house. After a few moments, the pair settled in each other's arms, talking quietly, discussing plans and excitedly wondering how they should break the news to Mary, the next morning. Emma knew her sister would be overjoyed with the news, perhaps almost as much as she herself was…

A NOTE FROM THE AUTHOR

Dear Reader,

Thank you for choosing to read my story… I sincerely hope it lived up to your expectations!

It gives me great pleasure to know that people are reading my books and delving into my fertile imagination. I love to write about the Victorian era, especially Victorian romantic novellas.

I enjoy looking into the historical lives of those who walked this earth before us, and finding out about the hardship's, trials and misfortunes they lived through and how they overcame these to fulfill their dreams.

I try to ensure that the story lines derived from these times are suitable for anyone and of any age.

Best Wishes

Ella Cornish

∼

Contact Me

If you'd simply like to drop us a line you can contact us at **ellacornishauthor@gmail.com**

You can also connect with me on my Facebook Page **https://www.facebook.com/ellacornishauthor/**

I will always let you know about new releases on my Facebook page, so it is worth liking that if you get the chance.

LIKE Ella's Facebook Page ***HERE***

I welcome your thoughts and would love to hear from you!

Printed in Great Britain
by Amazon